History Village:
The Cross Over

History Village: The Cross Over

Jo Elliott

History Village:
The Cross Over
© Jo Elliott 2018

Bible versions used...

- New International Version
- Contemporary English Version
- Good NewsTranslation
- King James bible
- The Living Bible
- The Message
- The New American Standard, New Testament Greek Lexicon
- Hebrew OT – Transliteration – Holy Name KJV, QBible
- Sharon Dingjan kindly assisted with the Hebrew translation

This book is a work of fiction. Named locations are used fictitiously, and characters and incidents are the product of the author's imagination. Any resemblance to actual events or places or persons, living or dead, is entirely coincidental.

Published by
Lighthouse Christian Publishing
SAN 257-4330
5531 Dufferin Drive
Savage, Minnesota, 55378
United States of America
www.lighthousechristianpublishing.com

"Walk about Zion, go around her, count her towers, consider well her ramparts, view her citadels, that you may tell of them to the next generation. For this God is our God for ever and ever; he will be our guide even to the end."
Psalm 48:12-14

CHAPTER 1: THE CAFE

The children had overheard their parents fighting before, but their Mum and Dad had always tried to explain away these arguments, saying they were merely "discussing" a situation. The children, however, recognised controlled anger when they heard it. It seemed to them that these "discussions" had been going on for quite a while now. Their Mother was *always* angry with their Father. Understandably, their Dad wasn't around as much as he used to be, driving home from work well after dinner every night.

Each of the children had developed a different way of dealing with the tension at home. Ally, thirteen and the eldest, attempted to block out her parents' arguments by lifting the volume of her IPod to as high as her eardrums would comfortably allow. She was not interested in listening to her Step-Mum's latest rant. In fact, she didn't really like Cassie, her Step-Mum; they had very little in common. Cassie was only interested in looking "hot" and dressing in clothes that were not really designed for *older* women. More importantly, Ally did not look like her Step-

Mum; Ally's hair was plain brown, not the creamy mix of golden blonde and white tones her Step-Mum demanded from her hairstylist.

Ally actually believed that her Step-Mum was embarrassed by Ally's appearance. Cassie would personally scrutinise each item of Ally's clothing, before Ally was allowed to leave the house. Her father must have noticed how much it "pained" Ally to have to undergo this ritual every day... but he chose to say nothing.

Josh, ten, would attempt to distract his parents, believing that if the adults had something different to focus on, they might forget about their issues with one another…Josh was getting quite good at applying the "distraction technique":

"Mum, can I order a caramel milkshake?" he interrupted her, knowing full well his Mum's abhorrence for sugary beverages.

Josh would have welcomed an angry retort from his Mother, if it meant that she would then stop hassling his Step-Dad. (Josh considered this an acceptable price to pay.) His Mother, however, was particularly angry today. She transfixed her steely gaze onto Josh for a brief second, just enough time to scold him for his bad food choices, before continuing her relentless tirade against her husband.

Great, Josh lamented inwardly. Now his Mum was angry with everyone, including him.

The family's Sunday brunch was not going well. They had all agreed to try out the newest local eatery called "The Church Café" to celebrate his Mum's fortieth birthday. However, instead of this outing helping to heal the family rift and improve things, it only seemed to intensify his parents' squabbles by shifting their argument into a public place.

This is turning into a "CWOT" (Complete Waste of Time), thought Josh miserably. Now everyone, including the waitress, could hear how horrible their family life really was…

It hadn't always been this way. When his Mum had first met Ally's dad, Brett, she had seemed so happy. She had laughed more, always dressed in her favourite tight blue jeans, and was generally nicer to everyone, including Josh. Back then, his Mum hadn't blown a fuse when Josh had admitted to having forgotten to brush his teeth (like what had happened on Friday morning at the school gate… in front of all the other schoolkids). Luckily, the kids who had overheard his Mum yelling were much older than Josh and in a different grade. (They still managed to have a bit of a chuckle, though, before heading off to their classroom.)

Brendan, four, was the youngest. Cassie had become pregnant with Brendan five years ago, prompting her to hurriedly marry Brett, and start their "new" family. In the space of one year, both Ally and Josh had gone from being "an only child" to having two other siblings. And it had taken some getting used to…

Ally didn't know anything about being the "older" sister, and didn't particularly care for the role. It seemed to her that Josh didn't really need her around anyway. He was a pretty good kid, on the whole. Josh tended to spend a lot of time on his own, reading and playing computer games, he cleaned his room when asked, and didn't cause much trouble for her.

The real truth was that Ally preferred to spend time with her friends at School, rather than with her family. Her school friends were fun to hang around with: they were always laughing at something (or someone). They were hardly ever serious. Bella and Maddie also had stories about their own families' strange behaviour. In many ways, School and the friendships she had formed there, had helped Ally cope with the arrival of a new Step-Mum and two younger brothers.

Ally's biological Mum had left when Ally was much younger (almost Brendan's age). Ally didn't like thinking about her real Mum. For the first few years after *it* had happened, Ally had wondered if she had been the real reason for her mother leaving…

Brendan suddenly became fidgety and decided he wanted to leave the table. The Café sat at the foot of a tall, bluestone cathedral, adorned with a metal cross on top. Brendan had seen other buildings marked with a cross, but he had no idea what they were like inside.

"Mum, can I please go and explore?" Brendan asked in his sweetest voice.

"I don't blame you," his Dad interjected. "In fact…Josh, Ally, why don't you ALL go and have a look around; we can order our meals when you get back." Their Mum bit her lip and glared at their Dad.

Before Cassie had an opportunity to rescind their father's offer, all three children hurriedly left the table and headed off in the direction of the church. Seven flat steps led from the café table onto a covered porch, which the children quickly traversed. From there a door opened into a double-nave with six tall vaulted bays.

"Awesome!" Josh exclaimed, as Brendan raced past him.

Inside, the building was even more impressive than the children could have imagined. The inner chamber was huge.

As the children paused to absorb their new surroundings, Ally noticed that the panel above the church's entryway was engraved with twelve vines and twelve bunches of grapes. She thought about the hours it would have taken for someone to chisel out those detailed carvings, and then paint them in different shades of red and green. (The colours had long since faded, but she could still make out the pretty design.)

The church also contained some beautiful paintings. One that caught Ally's eye was of a populated seaport with lots of fishermen either tending to their nets or examining their "catch". *My Art teacher at School would be really impressed*, she thought…

Two massive white pillars stood in the middle of the church like a central spine, supporting the six bays. Josh also noticed two stained-glass windows on the sides of each bay, a total of twelve windows, he quickly counted in his head. Each window seemed to be directing light to the front of the church. Without these windows, the church would have been in complete darkness.

Josh had never really liked the dark. Yet, this old building was not completely pitch black; the filtered lighting created just the *right* amount of mystery, he concluded. In some ways, the front of the church resembled his school's Assembly Hall, as there were several steps leading up to the stage area and lectern. *I guess people make speeches from up there,* Josh surmised.

There were also two round stained-glass windows on either side of the lectern; each window containing a picture of historical figures dressed in long, white robes. The men depicted in the window frame were turning askew, and gazing in wonder at a central male figure who sat elevated on a throne, resting in clouds (presumably in a galaxy somewhere). Right between these oval windows hung a wooden cross. The cross took up a lot of the wall space and looked quite ordinary, compared to the colourful windows and paintings adorning the other walls within the church.

As he looked at the cross, Josh was reminded of his Step-Dad. When Brett and Ally had first come to live with him and his Mum, Josh had helped his new Dad design and build an actual see-saw in the back yard, simply by using two planks of timber they had purchased from the local hardware shop. Josh really loved his see-saw.

He was also pretty impressed with his new Dad's skills. As it turned out, though, you really needed another kid to *work* the see-saw; Ally was certainly not interested in playing with him, and Brendan was far too little. Consequently, the see-saw had sat neglected in a corner of their yard. Since then, his Stepfather had also seemed to lose interest in Josh as well. Josh didn't know who his *real* Dad was. His Mother had never wanted to talk about his biological father, so Josh had stopped asking her questions about him.

Josh wondered if the wooden cross had something to do with that mythical figure called Jesus who had died thousands of years ago. Josh didn't know much else.

Both Ally and Josh suddenly heard the shrill scraping of metal, coming from somewhere inside the church. Josh looked around and realised that Brendan was missing…

"Ally, where's Brendan?" Josh asked tentatively.

"I don't know!" she snapped back.

Ally was really annoyed that she was expected to be responsible for Brendan. She had enough problems of her own to worry about, without having to concern herself with a four-year-old who was always running away and NEVER doing what he was told. Ally's school exams were in a few weeks, and she was falling behind in Maths. If that wasn't enough to worry about, there was also the end-of-year dance to think about. Some girls had already managed to secure "dates" to the dance, and excitedly bragged about which guy had asked them. With only a few weeks to go before this major event, there were three girls in Ally's class who had *not* been asked to the dance and Ally was one of them. In her mind, Brendan was definitely *"SEP" (Someone Else's Problem)*.

Josh and Ally walked towards the sound of the noise where they spotted Brendan in a tiny alcove, sectioned off from the main church. He was perched on top of a tall ladder, looking very small, but clearly quite elated with his climbing skills.

"Look at me!" he squealed.

"Get down, Brendan! You shouldn't be up there," Josh scolded him crossly.

This alcove was in a state of serious disrepair, with yellow tape separating it from the main church, clearing intending to bar people from entering. Brendan, however, had simply ignored the danger and climbed under the tape, before clamouring several feet off the ground and hanging off a ladder.

"If Mum saw you, you would be in a heap of trouble… you better come down right now!" Ally demanded. She made a mental note to *NEVER have children of her own; they were simply too much work.*

Brendan, however, had no intention of climbing down. Everything looked a lot more interesting from up above. He could see cobwebs and dead spiders adorning the cornices, crumbling stonework of various chunks and shades, missing stone sections and chiselled-out cavities. There was even a makeshift "ledge" with a hammer and a blade cutter simply resting on top of it. Brendan thought he could spend heaps of time exploring this exciting new world…

"Brendan! Come down NOW, or I swear, I'll go and get Mum!" Josh was becoming quite red in the face as it was clear to him that Brendan was not listening.

"In a minute…" Brendan retorted. Something had caught Brendan's eye in one of the wall cavities. It looked like a rolled-up piece of paper, wedged between two stones. The item rested innocently beneath the central arch, and definitely warranted further examination. Before the others could yell at him again, Brendan had turned his body ninety degrees, sidled as close to the wall as possible, reached across and simply grabbed it. At that exact moment, Ally and Josh both screamed as a whole lot of crumbling mortar and dust began to descend without warning, covering them both in old dirt and bits of plaster.

"Brendan! GET DOWN NOW before this whole place collapses!!!" Ally yelled, brushing the dust out of her hair.

She didn't know anything about stone foundations, but these crumbling mortar joints could not be a good sign…

Brendan, satisfied with the fruits of his labour, scurried down the ladder as quick as a flash, carrying his souvenir with him. He was eager to show the others what he had uncovered, and quite oblivious to the fright he had given them.

"Look what you've done! I'm covered in dirt!" Ally was furious with Brendan, and forcibly grabbed his hand, pulling him out of the alcove before the church ceiling could fall on top of them. (She had no intention of dying just yet.)

Josh's eyes moved from the crumbling ceiling to his little brother's delighted face, and thought about how different Brendan was from him. Josh would *never* have climbed anything that tall, for fear of falling and hurting himself. In fact, Josh didn't believe in taking any unnecessary risks. He was much happier reading about other people's adventures than experiencing his own. (It was safer that way, he reasoned).

CHAPTER 2: THE PARCHMENT

Brendan thrust the rolled-up bit of paper in front of his siblings' faces:

"Look what I've got!" he boasted, before finally handing it over to Josh.

Josh carefully took the frayed, yellowed paper from Brendan's excited clutches. It had been rolled up just like a scroll. As Josh examined it further, he realised that there was a lot of orange powdery residue coming away from the seal, leaving a bright orangey stain on his hands.

"This must be REALLY old. The ink is coming off," Josh reported, matter-of-factly.

Ally tried to look disinterested, even though she had learnt about scrolls in History class at School, and how people in ancient times had used scrolls instead of books. She recalled the teacher saying that the paper used for scrolls had come from the papyrus plant grown in Egypt. Ally wondered if this scroll was Egyptian, or just a fake...

"I'm going to rest it somewhere, so we can examine it properly," Josh told the others. Josh liked the fact that they trusted him with this important discovery. (He relished the responsibility.) As Josh moved towards the lectern, Brendan followed at his heels, skipping and jumping with excitement, impatient for news of what he had unearthed. Ally too walked in close succession behind the boys. She wondered if there was anything of importance written on the document. She had never read anything really old before.

Josh placed the scroll cautiously on the lectern. Part of him wondered if they should report their findings to their parents. Josh started to worry about whether they might get into trouble for breaking the seal, but as he touched the paper, he realised that the document's seal had already lost its adhesiveness – most of it was now just a mound of orange powder. As the seal had "kind of" already been broken, Josh rationalised that it might be ok to proceed…

"Open it, open it!" insisted Brendan.

"What do you think, Ally? Do you think we should? Josh asked timidly, wanting reassurance from someone older.

Ally was surprised that her opinion mattered to anyone.

"Whatever," she said, almost like it didn't concern her in the slightest.

The scroll actually reminded Ally of something she had seen before. She knew it was significant. *Oh yeah,* Ally suddenly recalled, turning to face the large painting, near the front door. It was a picture of God (she imagined) sitting on his throne, holding a similar looking scroll in his right hand. The scroll in the painting, however, was sealed in seven places. There was also a lamb standing in the centre of the picture, about to accept the scroll from God and open it…but the lamb looked injured. There was blood on its white woollen coat.

"I think scrolls are meant to be opened," Ally pronounced, trying to sound intelligent.

With that encouragement, Josh gently lifted the seal and proceeded to read the parchment aloud:

"I, the Master Builder of this Church pray for God's hand of blessing on all who enter her doors. May God's dominion, power, triumph, dignity, strength and glory rest on all of its inhabitants!"

Josh paused for a second and took a deep breath. He wondered if the Builder was talking about them.

"Josh, I think there's also something written on the back," Ally suggested, craning her neck to see.

Josh turned the delicate paper over. Something else had been added to the parchment, probably by another person as the writing now looked different…

"The Lord looks down from heaven on all mankind to see if there are any who understand, any who seek God…

The Lord is near to all who call on him, to all who call on him in truth.

He will fulfil the desire of those who fear Him; He also will hear their cry and save them!

The Lord watches over all who love him, but all the wicked he will destroy."

Josh stopped reading. The children looked at each other but didn't speak for a few moments. The message sounded scary…

"Do you think God is looking down on us right now?" Brendan asked his siblings, his eyes darting from one to the other in excitement.

Typical, thought Josh. *Brendan ignores the "wicked" bit and only thinks about the "good" bits.*

"That's what the scroll says," Ally replied matter-of-factly.

"How can we call him? Does he have a mobile we can ring?" Brendan asked naively. "I need to ask him to help me with my shoelaces…

and how to read… oh, and when I have bad dreams. Mum and Dad don't like it when I wake them up at night. They tell me to go straight back to bed, but sometimes I'm too scared to…" Brendan confessed shyly.

"God doesn't have an actual mobile you can ring, Brendan," Josh responded quietly. "I think it just means that if you really look for God, he can help you."

"Let's look for God, then!" Brendan exclaimed delightedly. "Where do you think he is?" Brendan started running around the stage area, trying to work out where God could be hiding…

"Brendan, God isn't really here on earth," Ally said, exasperation evident in her voice. However, when Ally saw the huge disappointment on Brendan's face, she quickly added: "He's probably in Heaven, waiting up there for us."

Brendan was not happy with Ally's response:

"But the paper said, that he's NEAR to those who call him, and that God can hear you when you call!" Brendan argued.

Brendan knew what he had heard, and he wasn't about to stop believing the promise that had been made.

"Maybe it means that if you concentrate REALLY hard and think about God, he will be close by…Perhaps he can read your mind or thoughts, or something…" Josh offered. Was this so far-fetched an idea? he thought to himself.

Josh had often (silently) hoped that God *could* help his family. His parents were either yelling at each other, or at one of the children. It actually felt like no-one in his family really cared about anyone else... Ally never talked to Josh about *anything*, and Brendan was too young to know how families should behave. There was literally NO-ONE Josh could turn to for help.

"Then let's all think about God," Brendan said. "We'll do it together, OK…? One, two, three, GO!"

Ally looked at the boys. They both suddenly acquired a really serious expression on their face, in their joint determination to *think* about God. Ally knew the idea was stupid. A long time ago, when she was little, Ally had actually believed in God. Recently, though, she had been far too busy simply trying to "survive" secondary school to think about God, or any Higher Power for that matter. The only time she heard God's name (or even "Jesus") being uttered was when people around her were really angry or just frustrated… Ally, too, used God's name when she was upset, even though she didn't *believe* in him.

"Ally, you've got to try too! Please?" implored Brendan.

Brendan wanted to ensure the success of his effort. He knew that God would be looking at Ally and wondering why she wasn't trying.

Ally thought about the pressures she was under at School and at home. She wasn't really enjoying life very much. Could it hurt to try this prayer (or sorts), and see what happened?
If God *could* actually hear her cry for help and save her from the times she felt unimportant … or just totally useless…perhaps something might change? (Ally would have given anything to be cooler, and thinner AND more confident… anything other than the person she saw in the mirror.)

They were all now united in their determination to seek God's help. Without further prompting, each child shut their eyes, and concentrated hard.

CHAPTER 3: THE LAKE

When they opened their eyes again, they glanced around, half expecting to see or hear someone in their midst. Everything, though, looked exactly the same. Without speaking, the eldest two started to make their way to the door, thinking it was time to return to the Café… almost like they had forgotten about the parchment.

"Mum and Dad will be waiting for us," Josh quietly reminded Brendan, who was still standing at attention.

Inwardly, Josh was feeling disappointed. However, he didn't want to let the others know *how much* he had been counting on this "call" to God.

"But we haven't seen God yet!" Brendan asserted. "We need to wait for him…"

"Brendan, c'mon. It's time to go," Ally repeated.

At this, Brendan's eyes started to fill with tears.

"But he promised!" Brendan reminded them. "A promise is a promise."

Josh took his hand and steered him out of the church. At this, Brendan started to whimper away quietly.

The sky outside was blue and cloudless, and dominated by a big hot sun which momentarily blinded all three children as they filed out of the church. They each wondered where all this light had come from. The sky was so much brighter than before…

Josh released Brendan's hand so that he could remove his jacket. He was feeling really hot and he wondered why the weather forecaster had got it so wrong today. Josh enjoyed listening to the weather reports each day, and had expected to see grey skies and cool temperatures.

As they continued to walk in the direction of their parents, Ally and Josh suddenly stopped. There were no chairs and tables set up outside the church. In fact, there were no waiters or waitresses serving food, no audible conversations…nor could the children hear clanging cutlery anywhere. The Café had simply vanished. More ominously, their parents were nowhere in sight.

"Josh, where are they?" Ally asked nervously. Her heart started to beat very quickly and her hands were becoming wet and clammy. The heat wasn't helping.

"I have no idea… I thought they were right here," Josh responded turning his head frantically, looking in every direction.

He started to think that perhaps the children had mistakenly come out of a different door… Their parents might simply be sitting around the corner, on the other side of the building.

Together, the children picked up their pace, and circled the entire boundary of the church building. Nothing looked familiar... All they could see were thick forests of pine and juniper and cypress. A mountainous hinterland lay before them, dotted with olive trees and grape vines. Where were the busy streets and the buildings, they wondered anxiously.

"Umm…where are we?" Ally finally asked, her voice quivering a little. (She hoped she was having some sort of bad dream.)

Josh walked towards a tall cedar tree and leaned against its thick trunk. He needed to figure this out, but he just couldn't think with the sun beating down on him. The evergreen tree was strong and tall, possibly over 120 feet in height. Its green leaves gave him (and a nest of chirping sparrows above him) some protection from the sun's scorching rays, but because the tree was so tall, its shade was limited to a small patch of grass.

The others soon joined him, also seeking reprieve from the heat. Together, the children just stood there, feeling confused… and frightened.

"Where the hell are we?" Ally reiterated.

Josh had no idea where they were, so he didn't answer her. He also didn't want to scare Brendan.

"Why don't we climb that hill? Perhaps we will see something familiar," Josh finally suggested.

Brendan reached the top of the hill first – all around were lush fields of greenery and wildflowers in bloom. Several high mountains could also be seen in the distance.

"Weeee!" Brendan squealed. He started skipping through the pastureland, pausing to look at the red lilies along the way. Some of the flowers were almost up to his waist. Brendan thought how much fun it would be to stomp on them… so he did. Very soon, a pleasing fragrance filled his nostrils.

"I can see water," Ally called out. She loved swimming in their pool at home, and had recently represented her school in a swimming carnival (but hadn't earned a ribbon, as pointed out by her Step-Mum). Sure enough, beyond the grove of cedar trees and prickly juniper shrubs the children could see the coast, with a busy commercial port in tow. There appeared to be people walking along the shorefront. Others were sailing in fishing boats that skimmed along like clouds. A flock of sea gulls was also noisily patrolling the port.

"Let's go for a swim!" Brendan shouted.

Josh strained his eyes to look at the port. He then looked back to see the church, trying to get his bearings. The church, however, was no longer in sight. It had vanished…

"We might as well head towards the water," Ally offered. "Perhaps we can find a phone, and ask Mum and Dad to come and get us?"

Ally was regretting leaving her handbag behind at the Café. She never carried much money with her, but her bag did contain her mobile phone, lip gloss, earphones, and hairbrush – all of the essentials, she thought.

As the children looked in the direction of the port, they noticed a stone-paved road which had been cut through the hills. This road appeared to connect up with the water, so they decided to follow it down. A little way along, though, the children came across some large wooden crosses standing eerily to one side of the road.

"That's weird….Don't crosses belong in churches?" Ally asked Josh.

Josh started to feel uneasy, but he thought it best to keep moving and avoid the sun's scorching heat. He was wearing his Nike cap, but he noticed that the others wore no hat and would soon get sunburnt.

"I'm starving," Brendan suddenly announced.

They should *all* have been enjoying their nice Café lunch, right about now, Josh thought miserably. However, instead of tucking into a cheese hamburger and French fries, the children were travelling down an isolated road with rocky soil and thorn bushes for company, to an unknown destination...

"Look at that tree," said Ally pointing to a leafy, olive tree on the side of the road. Ally thought how good its black olives would be to eat…

"I'm going to try some."

Ally loved olives in salads and was always grabbing as many olives as she could from the salad bowl at home. Before anyone could stop her, she went and plucked an olive straight off the tree, put it in her mouth, and then started coughing and spitting it out immediately.

"That's disgusting!" she yelled. "I think it's poisonous."

"It probably just hasn't ripened yet," Josh told her.

"No! I really think I have just poisoned myself," Ally argued, as she continued spitting out the olive remnants from her mouth. It tasted so bitter and horrible.

"Let's just keep going. We're almost there," Josh tried to lead the others, but they had stopped listening to him.

Ally was upset with Josh, complaining that "he didn't care about her near-death experience". And Brendan just kept moaning about being hungry.

When the children finally made it down to the water, they were far from happy, despite the gentle lapping sound of the waves and the cool breeze that was coming off the lake. Branches of surrounding palm trees swayed in easy formation as the sun shimmered on the expansive blue water in front of them.

The children temporarily forgot about their problems when they saw the vibrant activity happening on the shore. Men and boys of all ages, were calling out and signalling to each other as they collectively worked on their fishing vessels.

Built of mostly cedar planks, these flat-bottomed boats had been overturned on the hot sand, and were getting patched up. The boats were large, about thirty feet in length and eight feet in width. The children could see the exposed hulls and the various joints and nails; these boats had clearly withstood many repairs. There were also boats anchored in the water with hefty oars fixed in place for four staggered rowers. Their white lateen sailing masts were bobbing in the breeze, creating a quaint backdrop.

The smell of barbequed fish also permeated the air, and reminded the children of their most immediate problem. Following the source of this wonderful smell, they spotted three shirtless men sitting around a campfire. One man was using a stick from an oregano and hyssop plant and was poking at some fish as it lay simmering away on the fire's burning coals. He seemed to be testing to see if the fish was ready to eat, while his friends sat cross-legged, happily chatting to one another as they patiently waited to share in what promised to be a delicious lunch.

Before they could stop him, Brendan ran up to the men and asked if he could have some food. The men stared at Brendan and then at each other with confused looks. One of them responded in a language that did not sound like English. Ally and Josh quickly ran up to the men, and apologised profusely, before firmly steering Brendan away.

"Brendan, you don't ask people for food. And you NEVER speak to strangers!" Ally chastised him.

"But I'm starving!" he said clutching his stomach.

A few minutes' later, one of the men walked up to the children and offered them a woven basket containing three freshly caught, lemon-scented (perfect-looking) fish. There were also some warm bread loaves sitting alongside the fish. Ally just stared at the guy. He was around sixteen and incredibly cute. She had no idea what to say to him… Brendan, however, snatched the basket and began to rip into its contents. The handsome stranger just smiled and then returned to his friends.

Once seated, he looked back at Ally, for the briefest of looks.

CHAPTER 4: THE VILLAGE

Having devoured the contents of the basket and then licked their sticky fish fingers clean, the children decided it was time to look for a phone. They thought about asking to borrow one from the fishermen but these men had since returned to their boat and were busy working (at quite a frenetic pace). It seemed that everyone on the shore was fully immersed in the business of catching fish.

As they hadn't seen any shops along the shoreline, the children thought it best to try and locate a nearby shopping district. From the lakcfront, thcy had spotted another road, stone-paved and flanked by a footpath and a drainage ditch. Hopefully, it would lead them to the local shops, they thought wistfully. The children started to make their way towards it, but they soon came to an abrupt stop.

"Brendan, have you had another accident?" Ally enquired of the youngster, as the smell of poo began to fill the warm, salty air around them.

"NO!" Brendan replied, indignantly.

Brendan had been wetting his bed at home. Ally had overheard her Step-Mum imploring him to "Stop... now that he was four." Ally had felt sorry for Brendan at the time, but today, she was feeling less sympathetic, given the fact that they were nowhere near their home (and a supply of fresh underpants).

"You better not have…" she threatened.

"It's not Brendan... Look!" Josh called out, pointing to the nearby ditch.

Travelling down the drain, just alongside the road was filthy, brown-coloured water and slimy poo. It was flowing straight down to the lake.

"That's disgusting!" cried Ally. She thought she might be sick. "There's so much of it," she exclaimed, pinching her nostrils to try and block out the horrible fumes.

"We should just keep moving," Josh instructed. "This road has to lead somewhere."

Josh was fearful that they might never be able to locate a phone with which to contact their parents. He hadn't seen any overheard power lines anywhere…

"I need to 'go'," Brendan suddenly announced.

"That's great!" replied Ally, annoyed.

She looked around the olive groves and said testily:

"Well, there are no toilets here."

"You can probably 'go' over by the trees," suggested Josh. "Dad and I once pee-ed in the backyard. It's no big deal. I need to 'go' too…"

"Please show some RESPECT!" Ally said, looking mortified.

Once the boys had relieved themselves in the open countryside, the children continued their trek along the road. A short time later, they stumbled upon a busy marketplace filled with people haggling over all sorts of items displayed on wooden trestle tables. There were food stalls and measuring scales, pottery jars, and Aladdin-style lamps everywhere.

Ally's eyes were instantly drawn to the cloth materials and jewellery on sale.

"They're so cute," she said to no one in particular.

Individual shops appeared all along the main road, everything from bakers, butchers, money changers, farmers, even perfumers advertising their products. Traders *hinted* at their profession by wearing a symbolic item…

"Seriously?" Josh asked.

Some shopkeepers had placed wood chips behind their ears, others wore needles in their tunics… There were even some men donning small coloured rags. Ally assumed they were tailors.

In amongst the shoppers, the children could hear pigeons and chickens beating their wings against their wooden cages. There were donkeys, saddled and bridled, tied by ropes to nearby posts as they too watched the throng of activity. Strangely enough, no cars, motorbikes, or even push bikes were visible – only heavy-laden mules packed with goods, and the odd horse, dragging a cart. Lots of little children were happily playing together in the street, barefoot, adding to the noise levels and vibrancy. The children watched with particular interest when a guy tried to navigate his herd of sheep and goats along the narrow walkway, right past them.

"These people look a little creepy," Ally confided.

Wherever she turned, she noticed old men wearing ankle-length, loose woollen garments, held at the waist with thick leather belts. The men all had tanned faces and longish beards. *They could be terrorists,* Ally shuddered. Their heads and shoulders were covered with scarves… and they all wore brown, leather sandals, with no variation in style or colour. The women looked slightly more interesting, but even *they* looked weird, with veils covering most of their faces, only their eyes being visible.

As the children stood observing the crowd, various people passed by and began to stare at Ally. Some men had furrowed brows, and started pointing their finger at her. Ally was clearly becoming a source of escalating anger.

"I don't like it here. I think we better keep moving," Josh instructed the others.

Ally was just about to agree with her brother's assessment, when all of a sudden, an old man with a dark, wrinkly face walked right up to her, grabbed her bare shoulders and started shaking her vigorously and yelling something she couldn't understand. Ally screamed in horror. Brendan immediately began to kick the man as hard as he could. As he struck the man, the blue tassels attached to the four corners of the man's garment shook violently. Surprised by the sudden pain to his shins, the man released his grip on Ally for a brief second, giving her an opportunity to escape from under him… Ally then raced off, as fast as she could. Without a moment's hesitation, Brendan and Josh chased after her.

CHAPTER 5: LODGING FOR THE NIGHT

The children continued running until they sensed that the danger was over. They finally stopped at the foot of a nearby hill. They were all out of breath and panting furiously. Ally looked behind her and then at her brothers, and said:

"What the…??"

"I have no idea!" Josh replied, still trying to recover his breath. "Are you ok?" he asked with real concern.

Ally nodded, as tears started to fall from her eyes. She hadn't planned on crying, but the old man had given her one hell of a fright.

Brendan looked up at Ally, and reached for her hand. After a few seconds, Brendan asked Ally if he had "done good"?

"Yes, Brendan," Ally smiled. "That was really cool, what you did…"

Ally gave him a pat on his sweaty head. Brendan grinned back with obvious appreciation. (Ally hardly ever noticed him.)

At that moment, the children became aware of a solitary figure coming down from the hill above them. They looked up and noticed a man walking in a quiet, unhurried way through the rugged valleys. He was probably on his way to the market. There was nothing attractive about the man and the children wouldn't ordinarily have given this loner a second look. However, they were still "on edge" and needed to make sure that he was not dangerous, so they all turned round to face him…

In fact, they were so busy examining this man that they failed to notice the sound of angry male voices converging towards them, until it was too late. Suddenly, the mob of angry men with the long, flowing robes stormed right up to the children. Some of the men were now carrying heavy sticks as they began hurling abuse at Ally. One of them even started tearing at his own clothes in a dramatic gesture of pure hatred…

The children all started shuffling backwards –they couldn't run away, as the rocky hills loomed large behind them, blocking their exit. The men then began to encircle them like a pack of wild beasts. There was no way of escape.

Just then, the loner from the hilltop entered the circle, standing between the children and the angry mob. Ally could feel Brendan pushing up against her; he was clearly terrified by what might happen next… Ally's heart, too, was beating so loudly, she imagined everyone could hear it.

The loner said something to the men, which led to a heated argument. The children had no idea what was being discussed for everyone was talking in a foreign language... but it was clear that the loner was trying to stop the mob from doing something terrible to Ally.

In the middle of the argument, the loner removed his shawl which had been protecting his head from the sun, and brought it over to Ally. He then gently placed the material over her head and shoulders, before giving her a reassuring smile. The angry mob watched on in silence, as Ally was being "out-fitted" by this stranger.

The mob began to murmur amongst themselves and throw venomous looks at the loner. But then, amazingly (and unexpectantly) the men began to walk away. The danger appeared to be over… Ally and the boys could breathe normally again.

Once the mob was completely out of sight, the loner looked over at the children and motioned for them to follow him. They were so grateful for his help, they all complied without question.

After following the man along some pebbled streets, they finally came across a group of square buildings constructed with uneven boulders. The buildings looked like people's homes. They were all double-storeyed, each with its own outside staircase leading up to a flat roof. Despite their size, the houses looked a little primitive, as mud and smaller stones had been used to plug holes in their construction.

The loner stopped right in front of one of these houses, and the children could see straight into someone's window. Inside the house was a family sitting around a dinner table. The various members of the family appeared to have their eyes closed and were holding hands. The children could see a man's mouth moving, but of course, they could not hear what he was saying.

"What are they doing?" asked Brendan.

"I think they're praying," replied Ally.

"What's PRAY-EEING?" asked Brendan. To Ally's surprise, she suddenly recognised one of the house's occupants– it was the cute guy from the lake. At that exact moment, the family all opened their eyes. Sensing that they were being watched, the lake guy and everyone else turned their heads instinctively towards the window, and saw the children looking in at them. The man and woman then waved at the children's "guide". The loner smiled and waved back; he was clearly a friend of theirs. The woman then looked at the children and motioned for them to come inside.

The children looked at each other tentatively. They had no idea what they should do… until the loner went and opened the large, wooden-hinged door facing the street, and encouraged the children to enter.

After the children had filed in, Ally looked back; she wanted to personally thank the man for protecting her earlier. The loner, however, must have decided to continue his trek towards the Village... He was nowhere to be seen.

CHAPTER 6: THE FAMILY

Inside the doorway entrance, there was an open courtyard. A small group of women were gathered around an outdoor oven, chatting as their food was being cooked. Hearing the creak of the door opening, the women all turned around and smiled at the children, before resuming their conversation.

Small rooms appeared to lead off from this central courtyard, each with its own low, narrow door. The children proceeded to open the door belonging to the "family"… they then cautiously stuck their heads in, looking for the people they had observed from the street….

With some hesitation, the children entered the family's house. The living room was softly lit by several small lamps. A large chest sat in the middle of the room and appeared to "double" as the family's dinner table. Common household wares such as cooking pots, jugs, storage jars, bowls, and cups were scattered around the room.

The lake guy was sitting on a mat, positioned on the floor. He was resting his left elbow against the chest table, while the older man (who had been praying) sat reclining next to him.

They both wore a beard and even though they were now fully dressed, you could tell that both men were physically strong. A younger boy, about Josh's age, was also sitting around the chest table. He had black, curly hair extending well past his temples, and was beaming with joy as the sight of these unexpected visitors.

The kindly woman who had gestured to them, wore her hair in a loose bun, and began to hug each guest in turn. The children were not accustomed to so much affection and just stood there, a little embarrassed by her embrace. They were not sure what they should do… The "father" then spoke to them; his voice was a little rough-sounding, but it was clear that he was inviting them to sit down.

Josh noticed that the floor was just pounded earth. In fact, there was very little furniture in the entire room, and strangely, no paintings or pictures hung on the wall, only pots and bowls. *They must be very poor*, he thought. Notwithstanding the simple surrounds, a pleasing aroma of fish, flavoured with celery, mint and lemon juice was wafting through the entire room… Josh licked his lips. The family were clearly about to tuck into a delicious dinner.

The children sat down on the floor mats, positioned quite close together. The lady then presented her guests with a large bowl filled with cold water, and began to wash their hands for them. She then used a towel to dry them… Ally was a little surprised by this, but decided to go along with it as she had little choice. After the hand-washing, the lady placed a dinner bowl before each of the children, but didn't offer them any cutlery.

That's weird, Josh thought. The family were all using their hands to eat! This was probably just as well, he mused, as Brendan had not yet mastered the use of a knife and fork.

A large earthenware bowl sat in the centre of the table, filled with delicious, flattened fish, topped with a creamy yoghurt dressing. Brendan was thrilled when he tasted the fish and discovered that it had only a few small bones…and an easily removable spine.

The lady insisted that they also try some of her freshly-baked barley bread. A bountiful supply of olives, cheese, eggs, figs and grapes also adorned the table, and these were sampled eagerly by all three guests…along with a sip of drink from the pitcher of watered-down wine. Josh had tasted wine before (secretly, at his grandfather's house), but this was the first time he had been served a whole goblet full.

They must think we're older than what we look, Ally concluded silently.

Ally noticed that the family ate with their right hand only, dipping their fingers into the same common bowl as they reached for more food. It took a little getting used to for Josh, but it didn't take Ally long to master this technique.

The lake guy didn't speak at all during dinner; he seemed preoccupied with finishing his meal. The young boy and his father, however, were eager to engage the children in conversation. They looked a little disappointed, however, by their guests' inability to speak their language; Josh had to continually apologise for not understanding their questions.

Suddenly, the father pointed to himself and said "Av". The young boy then pointed to himself and said "JAY-cob" with a big grin on his face. They were introducing themselves. Ally then looked at the lake guy. He returned the look and said: "AAR-on". The father then took the woman's hand and presented her to the children and said: "Imma".

When all the children had formally introduced *them*selves, they continued to be accosted with offers of more food. Of course, all three politely complied. Very soon, their stomachs were happily filled…

When dinner was finally over, Imma rose to clear the table, and started washing the used bowls with the fresh water that was stored in a large jug near the door. Most of the family's jugs were modest stone vessels, either carved by hand or made with a simple instrument. Imma looked expectantly at Ally for a moment or two, but Ally did not move from where she was sitting. Neither did anyone else.

"Should we ask if they have a phone? It's getting really late…" Josh enquired of Ally.

"I can't see any handsets anywhere," Ally responded. "I've got a feeling this town might be too remote for mobile use…but we could ask, I guess."

Josh looked at Av and began to mimic someone talking on a phone, while at the same time, asking him in a loud voice, "If he owned a telephone." Av, however, looked puzzled, and responded with a few questions of his own, all of course, in a foreign language.

"This isn't helping," Ally grimaced. "What are we going to do?"

She and Josh exchanged worried looks.

Imma pointed to the window, and then said something to her husband. There were no curtains on the window and it was getting quite dark outside. Av and his sons stood up and began to wipe the washed bowls, and tidy up. Av then spoke to the children and indicated that they should follow him. The children got to their feet and followed the family through to a smaller back room which looked very much like a stable.

"This smells foul," Ally winced, as she was suddenly overcome with the smell of wet fur, compounded by the odour of animal poo…

At the back of the tiny stable, the children could see a wooden ladder, which the family began climbing. The children followed closely behind, and pretty soon, they all stood in what appeared to be the family's sleeping quarters. Av and Imma started to unroll two long mats and place them sequentially along the floor.

Imma then took Josh's hand and encouraged him to follow her sons up to yet another level. When they got to the "roof", Josh could see the family's laundry in one corner, flapping in the gentle warm breeze. Also tucked away in a separate part of the roof were some fishing nets. These were hanging against a low wall, along with thick ropes and heavy-looking weights resembling black olives.

While the children looked on, Imma began to collect the laundry, which had long since dried. Av started unrolling one more mat which he and Aaron then placed on an empty section of the roof.

"I think YOU will be sleeping up here with the boys," Ally whispered to Josh.

Ally suddenly cringed when she realised that she was probably expected to sleep on the floor below…*with the parents*. Ally was not excited about the prospect of sharing a room with virtual strangers… plus a brother who occasionally wet himself, but she just bit her lip and said nothing.

Josh immediately began to explore the roof and was delighted with his accommodation. Even though the roof was open to the elements (and it was now practically night-time) the outside air temperature was lovely and warm. There were even guard rails placed all around the roof, to prevent anyone from falling down and hurting themselves. The best thing about the roof, however, was that you could see the night sky from up here… *You can study the constellations, without having to leave your bed,* Josh thought excitedly.

"How AWESOME!" he exclaimed.

The only "bummer" he discovered was that the toilet was situated *outside* the house. Before going to sleep, Imma asked Jacob to take all three children outside, and show them how to use the shovel to cover up the pit… after it had been used.

CHAPTER 7: NORTHERN LIGHTS

A half an hour later, Josh was lying flat on his back, on his new bed mat. Before disappearing downstairs, Imma had offered Josh a woollen cloak to use as a blanket. The coat was large enough to cover Josh comfortably, and he was really enjoying camping "outdoors". Aaron had fallen asleep instantly and was beginning to snore a little, while Jacob, continued chattering away about something or other… He was clearly stoked to be having a sleep-over.

As Jacob prattled on, Josh started counting the stars. From his home in Melbourne, Josh could usually count around one hundred stars. Tonight Josh could see even more bright lights than ever before. *It must be the unpolluted country air*, he concluded happily... *This is SO cool.*

A recent school visit to the planetarium had taught Josh about the star constellations of the Zodiac. He was amazed to learn how different stars could be seen during the year in different places, as the Earth orbited around the Sun and the seasons changed.

From the southern hemisphere, where he lived, Josh could see the Carina constellation, known as "the Keel". This, he learnt, was the bottommost part of old ships…kind of like the U-shape boats he had seen at the lake earlier in the day.

His favourite constellation, though, was "the Crux", or the Southern Cross because of the cross formation made by the four brightest stars… (Josh always thought it looked more like a kite.) The Crux was surrounded by Centaurus, "the Centaur", which resembled a half-man, half-horse creature. According to the expert at the Planetarium, legend had it that Centaurus first grouped the stars into constellations and helped guide a group of sailors called the Argonauts to read the night sky, by placing a picture of himself in the sky. Josh thought star-gazing "ruled."

However, tonight, as Josh studied the stars, something was not right. The Crux was usually his starting point, as it had always been used by explorers of the southern hemisphere to point south. For the first time *ever*, Josh couldn't find it.

What he could see, though, were seven bright stars that looked very much like "The Big

Dipper". He continued to stare at the dark sky... Josh thought he could actually see a flat "W" pressed against the Milky Way. *Is that Cassiopeia? Seriously?* Josh rubbed his eyes. These constellations shouldn't be here. They belonged in the Northern Hemisphere. He really wished he could *Google* this... Very soon after that, Josh fell asleep.

The next thing he knew, it was morning. Josh lay still for a minute, trying to remember where he was... He could hear chickens clucking nearby, and cows mooing as they waited to be milked. Josh suddenly remembered the previous day's events with a jolt. He looked around for Jacob and Aaron but they weren't there. He was beginning to feel very uneasy...

Josh got up from his makeshift bed, and went to look for his brother and sister. He found them both downstairs, busily munching away on breakfast. Breakfast turned out to be a smaller meal than the night before, but judging from their contented looks, just as enjoyable, with fresh warm bread, plump, juicy olives, and creamy goat's cheese on offer.

"Where have you been?" Ally asked Josh between bites. "You won't believe what *I've* been doing," she droned on without waiting for Josh to respond.

While Ally was telling Josh about having been woken up to milk the cow (before the sun had even risen), Josh could see Imma kneading bread in the corner. Jacob was standing in front of his Mother, reciting something out loud to her, from memory.

Jacob looked a bit "geeky" this morning, as he was wearing a pair of blackened square cases with straps attached to both his head and left arm. When he had completed his recitation, Josh watched as Jacob proceeded to put little bits of parchment back into the square black cases, before Imma gave him a huge hug (and covered him with flour, as a result of her bread-making activities). Imma and Jacob both laughed heartily at the mess they had just created.

Josh couldn't help thinking about his own Mum at that moment. *She wouldn't be laughing if flour had covered her clothing...or her clean floors*, he believed.

After Josh had eaten a little breakfast, Jacob urged him to come outside. Jacob was pacing around the kitchen impatiently and pointing to the door, all the while talking about something (incomprehensible to Josh).

Josh, however, wanted to talk to Ally and tell her about the "discovery" he had made last night.   She needed to know about the star constellations and what they meant…   Imma, however, had other plans for Ally. Once everyone had finished eating, Imma gently took Ally's arm and asked her to help with the washing.   Ally reluctantly got up, sensing that *more* work was required of her.

"Ok," she said dispassionately, trying to suppress a yawn.   Ally was accustomed to sleeping in on weekends… sometimes till midday. (On really good days, Ally would only get up to have some breakfast, and then go *back* to bed.)

"Ally," Josh said with a serious expression.

"YO," she responded without looking at him.

"I think we're really far from home," Josh whispered conspiratorially.

"No kidding, Einstein," Ally replied sarcastically.   "Brendan could have worked that one out."

"No, I mean REALLY far from home.   I think we're in a… different country!" Josh blurted out.

CHAPTER 8: THE PICNIC

It was clear that Ally was not in the mood for a sensible discussion. In the interim, Imma had managed to produce a basket of wool and was now trying to get Ally's attention, as she picked through threads, explaining the process of *working* the wool. Ally did not look impressed.

Jacob, too, was getting impatient with Josh – he was really wanting to go out. Josh finally decided to give up on Ally, and follow Jacob outside. Brendan quickly joined them.

Once outside, Brendan started jumping and running, clearly excited about the prospect of exploring his new neighbourhood. Josh, however, stood very still as he looked about him. There were women carrying water jars as they walked past the house at an unhurried pace. Some ladies were even walking with bundles of goods balanced on their heads. Mothers were sitting on their front steps, nursing babies in their arms. Two men and a teenage boy were passing along the rocky outskirts of the Village with a flock of noisy sheep. Not far away, an old man was sitting serenely in the shade of his doorway, watching the passing parade.

Jacob began drawing on the ground and numbering two rows of squares; in total, he drew four in a row.

I think he wants to play hopscotch, Josh deduced. Jacob then began to demonstrate the rules to his new friend, by hopping on one foot, and kicking a stone from one square to another. *His version requires a lot more skill than the one back home...*

Brendan immediately wanted to have the first "go". However, when he mistakenly placed his feet on the ground, Jacob began to remonstrate, as you weren't allowed to have *both* feet touch the ground... At that point, Jacob asked Brendan to stop playing and allow someone else to try. Brendan, however, didn't understand that he was "out", and refused to leave the game.

Great, thought Josh. *Jacob's going to get really mad now...*

Josh, however, was wrong. Jacob just laughed and allowed Brendan to try again.

As they continued to wait for Brendan to improve his technique, the children could hear people entering the street. Looking around them, they saw a sizeable crowd made up of men, women and even children, coming towards them and making a loud racket. Jacob recognised a "mate" in the crowd and went and asked him where they were heading…Jacob then ran inside and begged Imma to let him join the group. Imma came out of the house to see what all the commotion was about.

The crowd appeared to be heading towards the lake. Imma said something to Jacob, who followed her back into the house. When they both re-emerged, there was a satchel for Jacob, filled with fish and fresh barley loaves, and another satchel for Josh, packed with raisins, figs and a couple of apples.

"Thanks Imma," Josh said, appreciatively.

"Hey, that's not fair! You're going on a picnic… and I have to work," complained Ally who had come outside to see what was going on.

Imma then went up to Ally and gave her an affectionate squeeze around her waist, before placing one arm around Ally's shoulders. With her other hand, Imma grabbed Brendan, before he disappeared into the massive throng of people. (Imma had a loving way about her, which Ally and Brendan were instinctively drawn to.)

Meanwhile, Jacob and Josh followed the crowd, which only grew larger as more and more people excitedly joined them. *I wonder if we're going to swim at the lake,* Josh pondered.

He wasn't a fast swimmer. His Mum was adamant that he needed to practise more, in anticipation of the next School swimming competition. (She herself couldn't swim that well, but that didn't make Cassie any less demanding in her expectations of her son.)

Soon after arriving at the lake, the boys saw that thousands of people were already there. The crowd began sitting on the grass, like they were waiting for something... Some people were calling out the name "Rabboni". Everyone kept their eyes glued to the lakefront.

Perhaps they've all come to see a show, and the performers are arriving by boat, imagined Josh. Sure enough, a boat was steadily making its way to the shoreline. When it moored, everyone's attention was fixed on the men who climbed out of this boat. The men then walked up the side of the mountain, to the very top of the hill.

"We can see everything from here," Josh announced to Jacob.

From their vantage point, the boys could observe the men quite clearly. The performers didn't look that interesting though, Josh thought. They were just wearing the same long-flowing, belted gowns (like everyone else). They carried no musical instruments or props of any kind. *I wonder what they're going to do,* he pondered.

Just then, "the Main Man" began addressing the entire crowd. *That must be "Rabboni,"* (the name people were chanting before) Josh concluded.

There was absolute silence as Rabboni began to talk. There were no interruptions at all, not even the sound of a baby crying… The crowd was listening carefully to every word this Rabboni spoke.

Josh looked around him. The audience seemed surprised at what Rabboni was saying but they remained perfectly still, eager to hear more. Rabboni spoke with authority, like someone who knew what he was talking about. He did not shout, and surprisingly, the people could hear every word.

Josh wished he could understand what Rabboni was saying, but it was not in English. To Josh, Rabboni looked a little bit like the loner the children had met yesterday. (Josh couldn't be sure, though, as Rabboni was on a hill-top, so far away from him.)

Josh's mind inevitably drifted to food and the fact that it had been *ages* since breakfast. He rubbed his stomach and suddenly remembered the lunch that Imma had packed for them.

Cool, he thought excitedly. *I can at least eat while Rabboni talks...*

Just as Josh was about to ask Jacob to open his satchel, Rabboni stopped talking and began to confer with the men standing closest to him. The men then began to survey the crowd, before looking back at Rabboni, and shaking their heads. *Something must be wrong*, thought Josh. Just then, Jacob grabbed Josh's hand and started leading him forcefully up the hill, towards Rabboni…

The boys had to carefully weave their way between all the people and jump over lots of legs, trying their hardest not to trip. *Jacob must really want to hear what's going on*, Josh reasoned.

When the boys finally got to the top of the hill, Jacob crept around, listening to the adults' conversation. He then approached one of Rabboni's friends and asked him a question. Without waiting for his response, Jacob removed the lunch satchel from his shoulder and simply handed it over to this man. He also tried to hand over Josh's satchel, but Josh resisted, holding on tightly to the leather strap.

"What are you doing?" Josh cried out. "I need this. I'm starving!"

The man took Jacob's satchel, while Josh just gawked at Jacob.

"Why did you give away our lunch? What are WE going to eat now?" Josh asked him, annoyed.

He couldn't believe what Jacob had just done. *At least we still have the apples and raisins,* Josh reminded himself.

Jacob, though, had his eyes fixed on Rabboni. Jacob's satchel was being handed over to Rabboni, who was now opening it and peering inside.

Rabboni then asked the men to arrange the crowd in a particular formation. Once all the people were sitting in rows (in groups of around fifty) Rabboni took Jacob's bread loaves and fish, looked up, and said something. He then broke the bread and handed it over to his friends, and asked them to pass it on to the people seated. He did the same with the fish.

Eventually, a man approached Jacob and Josh and offered them some of Imma's bread and fish. Josh thanklessly accepted a couple of the salted sardines, which tasted really good. When he later nibbled on some of Imma's bread, Josh glanced over at Rabboni.

It was definitely him. Rabboni was the guy who had given Ally his shawl.

After everyone had eaten all they wanted, Rabboni's friends started picking up the leftovers – unbelievably, there were twelve large baskets full of uneaten food. Jacob did not seem surprised at this. He did, however, look a little disappointed with Josh, who was still clutching his satchel, filled with only a handful of raisins, a few figs and two apples… but he said nothing.

CHAPTER 9: THE NEXT DISCOVERY

When the picnic was over, Rabboni and his friends came down the mountain, and got back into their boat to set sail across the water. The crowd then began to disperse.

As Josh and Jacob started walking back home, Jacob could not stop talking. Josh gathered that his friend was excited about how their lunch had actually fed thousands of people…

Josh, however was very quiet in comparison. He wondered if Rabboni had performed some kind of magic trick so that the food could just multiply… Or maybe, Josh was simply imagining all of this, and he would soon find himself back in Melbourne. He really needed to speak to Ally, he decided.

Back in the Village, Ally had had her own adventures. Once Jacob and Josh had left for the picnic, she had helped Imma bake some risen bread dough in the large communal oven, and had been instructed on the importance of keeping the fire going at all times. This was vital, it turned out, as the oven's heat, not only cooked the family's dinner, but it also supplied heating for everyone's home.

Ally had been introduced to the other women in the courtyard, who had warmly welcomed her into their group while they chatted (non-stop). Ally had become "accepted" by the women in no time at all. Brendan too had spent his day happily playing with the other young children in the courtyard, under the careful watch of all the mothers present.

Imma had also shown Ally how to prepare a lentil stew with vegetables and olives. As it turned out, cooking with Imma was fun. Imma was a patient teacher, and was constantly asking Ally to smell each fresh ingredient before adding it to the pot. The two of them had spent time tending the vegetable patch outside in preparation for the meal, and Ally had learnt how to pick various herbs, like dill and cumin, to flavour the stew. Imma was so pleased with the end result that she gave Ally a great big hug and paraded her proudly before the other women, all the while, explaining to them what an amazing soup Ally had created. Imma was beaming with pride.

Ally didn't think that the stew was *that* great. She was actually a little embarrassed by all the attention Imma was giving her. Ally couldn't help but compare Imma with her Step-Mum who had NEVER been proud of anything Ally had made.

The toughest job for Ally that day had been hauling water back from the wooden treadmill. Imma had shown Ally how to walk on the water wheels, which would cause the wheels to spin around, scooping up water into jugs as they went. The jugs would then drop into a sluice which filtered into a pipe, allowing the local women to collect clean water in their jars. It was up to Ally and Imma, however, to cart the heavy jars all the way back home, and dump the water into the courtyard cistern, allowing everyone in the courtyard to use it. *So much effort, just to get some water,* Ally sulked.

She also didn't enjoy wearing the veil to cover her head when she stepped outside…but she did not want to risk an altercation with that angry mob again, so she kept the head-covering on.

What Ally had really wanted to do all day was spend time with the family's animals, but there was never any free time. After *milking,* Imma had taken the cow and the mule out of the house and had tied them to the post outside. The animals seemed to know Imma and they responded obediently to her voice, while glancing shyly at their new visitor...

When she had been younger, Ally had wanted to be a vet, but quickly realised that you needed to get really good grades to qualify. She then "cancelled" this dream. Ally didn't believe in working that hard.

When the boys returned home from their picnic, Josh immediately went to look for Ally. He found her with Imma, washing clothes outside:

"Come inside, quickly. We need to talk," he interrupted.

Ally was not unhappy about stopping work, and turned to Imma to explain that she had to take a break. Imma looked a little puzzled, before nodding to Ally and continuing to rub away at the dirty clothes.

Ally followed Josh up to the roof, where they sat down on the beams. Josh took a deep breath before beginning:

"Listen, I have been thinking about everything that's going on here... I don't know where we are, and what's happening to us...and I have NO idea how to get back home. Ally... I'm really scared."

Ally looked into Josh's frightened face and then across at their surroundings. She peered over the wall and into the nearby hills. Where *would* their help come from, Ally thought anxiously.

"Hey, bro, I actually haven't had any time to think about it today, or yesterday (for that matter) …and I'm SO tired! Imma woke me up before freakin' dawn."

Ally didn't want Josh to know that she too was scared. Brendan suddenly appeared on the roof, munching on a fig. He pushed his little body in between them, and sat down, looking from one sibling to the other.

"What are you two doing? Do you want to come and play with me?" Brendan asked hopefully, showing them one of Jacob's toys.

Josh liked the look of the "archer" and the "soldier" action dolls with their little spears and bows and arrows. The toys appeared to be made out of clay and had accompanied Brendan everywhere in the last two days.

"Brendan, we can't play now. We're having a serious conversation. We're trying to figure out where we are AND what to do about it," Josh asserted with a worried look on his face. (Josh was starting to think that there was little point in "sugar-coating" the situation just because

Brendan was little. This problem would affect him too.)

"I already know the answer to that!" Brendan retorted smugly. "God is somewhere here. Remember when we all shut our eyes and did what the paper said to do? Well, God brought us HERE so that we can find him… I reckon he must be really close by!"

Ally and Josh stared at Brendan for the longest time…

CHAPTER 10: THE MAIN MAN

Aaron and Av had arrived back home satisfied with their day's catch, and in desperate need of a wash to get rid of the stench of fish. The men appeared to work in partnership, which suited Imma as she could plan the evening meal to correspond to a time when all her family were ready to sit down together and eat.

Before arriving home, though, Av and Aaron had spent time repairing and cleaning their fishing nets, which they could then hang on the roof of their home to dry before the next day's use. Av really enjoyed this quiet time with his eldest son, as it gave him a chance to talk to Aaron about the "trade"…just as his father had done with him. Father and son would discuss how many of each type of fish they had caught that day, and what kind of money they would fetch. The fishing business was hard work, but it certainly provided a decent income for the family, plus fresh fish to eat each day.

In addition to knowing how to fish, Av needed to speak several languages in order to sell his fish to merchants from far-off cities. Aaron, too, was becoming fluent in different languages simply by listening to his father transacting with foreigners. Aaron knew how to speak Hebrew, Aramaic and some Greek, but he did not know how to speak Ally's language. It sounded so different to anything he had ever heard. Aaron wondered where Ally came from… He had noticed that she wore a necklace which had a picture of islands in the sea. It reminded Aaron of a song he had learnt once, about *people in far-away places*…

Just as Aaron was going up to hang the nets on the railing, Ally was suddenly climbing down the wooden ladder. Aaron moved aside, graciously. Ally turned bright red as she ventured down the steps.

"Thanks, so much," she murmured.

When Ally finally made it to the bottom, there was not a lot of room to move around the landing. Aaron was now very close to her. He smelt of fish, but in a manly sort of way that she didn't object to. Aaron hovered for a bit, giving himself enough time to look into Ally's eyes. He noticed that they were a soft brown colour with yellow specks around the edges.

Just then, Josh and Brendan decided to climb down the steps, and Aaron was forced to move out the way. The "moment" was broken…

and Ally and Aaron soon headed off in opposite directions.

Later, Imma called all the family to dinner and they each took their place around the family chest table. (As it was getting late, the children had decided to look for "God clues" the next morning.) The sweet fragrance of the whole-wheat lentil casserole filled the entire house, and the children couldn't wait to get "stuck into it". Brendan was gently reprimanded by Imma when he started to eat *before* Av had finished giving thanks to God…

After dinner, Av pulled out a board game which looked very much like checkers. Aaron and Jacob played the first game, giving Josh and Brendan time to observe and learn the "rules". Imma cleaned the cups and bowls, while Av chatted to his wife.

Ally looked around at each of them and couldn't believe that all of this family activity was going on in such a small space. Back in Melbourne, they all usually went their separate ways in the evening: her brothers (she imagined) played computer games in their own rooms; Ally *Snapchatted* her friends (usually before starting on her homework); her Step-Mum watched cable television, while her Dad read a book in a different part of the house. No-one ever spent time together or even hung out in the same room.

Ally really missed her phone. She hadn't opened her Snapchat, or "liked" or commented on the Instagram posts of her friends in over a day. *What would they think of that? Surely, they will realise that I'm missing...*

The next morning, after breakfast, Ally waited until Imma was hanging the washing upstairs, before covertly sneaking out of the house with Josh and Brendan.

"Did you tell Imma we're going out for a bit?" Josh asked.

"Nope," answered Ally.

Imma would never understand what they were proposing to do, so Ally had decided it was pointless to try and explain… Adults never really understood ANYTHING. (Ally was actually hoping they would find their way back to Melbourne soon, in which case, they would never need to offer an explanation for their absence.)

When the children started out on their search, it was a fine day, full of promise. They had no fixed agenda but they kept their eyes open, looking for clues or signs from God...

"Look, at that building!" Josh exclaimed, his eyes drawn to a magnificent-looking temple in the centre of the Village. An imposing structure stood imperially behind a large open courtyard with colonnaded porticoes on two sides, and a porch entryway facing the street.

"That's so hard core," Ally replied. "We should definitely start there…"

As the children were about to climb the steps leading up to the building, they noticed the solid timber double doors barring the entrance to the Temple. A group of men were removing their shoes as they prepared to go through these doors, when suddenly, a scuffle broke out. (It appeared that one guy was trying to prevent another man on crutches from entering the building…)

The "fight" quickly escalated when it was apparent that the injured man was determined to go in, despite the opposition he faced. The men's voices started getting louder and angrier, and without warning, they began to shove and punch each other.

Suddenly, the man on crutches lost his balance and toppled over, screaming at the top of his lungs as he began falling down the steps…his crumpled body finally landing right on top of Brendan. Brendan fell backwards from the impact, and began howling in pain as his head hit the ground.

Horrified, Ally tried to lift Brendan from under the weight of the injured man, but she couldn't manage it... The man winced in pain as Ally tried to manoeuvre Brendan from under him. All the while, Brendan kept screaming in a high-pitched voice. Josh just stood there, frozen with fear.

At that very moment, a strong pair of arms appeared from nowhere, and gently lifted Brendan from beneath the man, before placing him a little further away. Some other people began helping the injured man who was bleeding. (The crutches were of little use to him now, as he was unable to stand.)

The kind stranger who had helped free Brendan, then said something to the children, before picking up Brendan again and carrying him away.

"HEY! Where are you taking him?" Ally screamed, giving chase.

Josh could not believe what was happening. He started running after both Ally and the man carrying Brendan…

It was only when they reached a crowd in the middle of an adjoining street that the stranger finally stopped running. In the centre of the crowd, stood Rabboni. Next to him, were his friends from the picnic.

Everyone was now looking at both the stranger, carrying a wailing child, and Ally, shouting at the top of her lungs to "STOP"! The loud commotion quickly unsettled the babies and the small children gathered, who frightened by the sudden disturbance, began to cry too.

Rabboni's friends immediately started to rebuke the parents for allowing their children to behave this way. Rabboni, too, looked angry. But he wasn't angry with the parents, or the children... Instead, Rabboni started telling off his friends. They lowered their heads, in shame.

Rabboni then placed his hands on Brendan's head, gently stroking the sides of his face and comforting him. Brendan looked up at Rabboni with his tear-stained face, and his sobbing began to dissipate. Within seconds, Brendan's fear and trembling had disappeared.

CHAPTER 11: UP A TREE

Upon their return, Imma and Jacob met the children outside the house. Imma was clearly very distressed by their disappearance. Her brow was furrowed as she began gently chastising them and waving her finger about…but surprisingly, she also seemed relieved to see them back.

She took Brendan's hand and led him inside, looking for a treat to give him. Brendan was soon trying to fit an entire delicious date in his mouth. This "feat" helped him forget all about his awful experience earlier that day.

Imma then looked across at Ally and attempted to draw her into a conversation about *where* the children had been all day. Ally was still traumatised by what had happened and was in no mood for a lecture by someone else's mother. Without providing a single word of explanation, Ally just left the kitchen and went upstairs (even though she knew it would be hotter there). Imma stared at the back of her, confused by Ally's behaviour. Imma hesitated for a moment, before deciding to follow Ally upstairs, and to continue the discussion there.

Jacob also wanted to know where Josh had been, and began launching a barrage of questions at him (oblivious to the fact that Josh had no idea what was being asked). It appeared that Jacob had made plans for the day…just for the two of them, but all of his great ideas had come to nothing when Josh had gone missing. Jacob decided to never let Josh out of his sight again.

The next morning, he woke Josh up by poking him in the belly. Opening his eyes slowly, Josh saw a grinning Jacob hovering over him. The sun was already out, with few clouds in sight. *The day's perfect for exploring,* Jacob thought excitedly, as he encouraged his friend to hurry up and get ready.

"Let me sleep!" Josh complained.

Privately, Josh had hoped that when he next opened his eyes, he would mysteriously find himself back in Melbourne… Jacob, however, would have none of it. He was determined to make the most out of the day, and wouldn't leave Josh alone. So, after a quick breakfast, Jacob led a grumpy Josh out of the house and down a rocky pathway, towards the town centre.

"Where are we going?" asked Josh as they passed the Village shops, which were already in full swing with people buying and selling. Jacob chattered away in response as they headed south towards the rich forests and farmlands. It was the beginning of the harvest and the labourers were out, beating olives off their trees and onto some nets sprawled across the dirt. There were also lots of women working in the nearby fields, picking grapes off the heavy vines.

The boys passed an old farmer resting under a sycamore tree. He was clearly overheated from his morning activity and squinted at the boys as they passed his land. He waved at Jacob, who waved back, and the boys continued on their way. They then passed farming land where old women could be seen gathering the cut grain that had been left behind by the reapers.

When the boys got to a water fountain, they stopped and looking longingly at the water which the locals were pouring into jars. A girl about Josh's age kindly offered them a drink from her water jar, having noticed that the boys had no jar of their own.

"Thanks," said Josh, unsure of what else to say.

She just laughed. The girl had long, dark hair and a nice smile, despite a few missing teeth.

The boys quickly finished gulping down the refreshing water before moving on.

A little way further, they approached a township which looked dry and arid. As the boys walked through the outskirts of this town, they could hear a man calling out… When they got a little closer to the town square, they realised that all the yelling was coming out of an old man, who was sitting alone on the side of the road:

"EESOOS! EESOOS!" he called to anyone who passed by.

"Let's cross to the other side," suggested Josh, thinking that the man might be dangerous.

Jacob, though, seemed unconcerned and walked right in front of the old man…who then reached out and grabbed Jacob's foot. Both boys jumped with fright… but as they looked down at the man, they realised that he was blind. His eyes looked really weird – they were yellow in the centre, and filled with a dense and cloudy substance. Josh had never seen a blind person before. (The man also looked like he hadn't eaten for a while; he was so thin...)

Jacob quickly said something to the blind man, prompting him to release his foot. The blind man then turned his head in the other direction, as if he was waiting for someone… Josh too looked around and noticed that a crowd of people were coming their way, all talking excitedly about something.

The crowd began to line both sides of the road, like they were getting ready for a parade. Pretty soon, Jacob and Josh could not see very much at all – there were so many heads in the way. There was, however, a fig tree not far from where they stood and Jacob started to make his way towards it. Josh instinctively knew what his friend was thinking…

"I'm not sure I can climb that," he confessed to Jacob.

Josh remembered the *Tree Adventure* obstacle course he had visited last year for a friend's birthday party. Josh discovered that he didn't have an actual fear of heights… just a fear of falling.

"We should probably inspect the tree carefully to see if it's safe for climbing," he added.

Josh began checking the tree, and believed that he would definitely need Jacob's help for his first footing. While he was thinking about whether his shoes had sufficient traction or whether he should attempt it barefoot, Jacob had already scrambled up the trunk. Two seconds later, Josh heard a scream.

Josh looked up, thinking that Jacob had climbed onto a branch that was breaking off or had snagged in the tree. But no…Jacob was perched securely on a sturdy branch, but he was not alone. There was a man sitting on a branch just above Jacob, and he looked mean.

CHAPTER 12: THE EAGLE HAS LANDED

The fierce-looking man was sitting high up, his body perpendicular to the trunk, leaving his legs free to kick Jacob. Jacob desperately began reaching for a lower branch in order to lower himself down, away from the man's violent strikes.

Josh did not know what he should do... He was wavering between climbing up the tree to help Jacob improve his grip, or just staying put, and being on the ground to help slow Jacob's descent in case he was pushed off. Tormented by his indecision, Josh cried out to the ruthless man:

"Hey YOU! Stop it! Can't you see, he's going to fall?"

Jacob had no time to test his footholds. He simply hugged the tree as best he could and quickly slid down. Once both Jacob's feet were firmly planted on the ground, the boys could hear the man laughing his head off.

Josh could not believe it. Jacob could have died, and this man thought it was hilarious! Jacob shook his fist at him, but Josh simply glared at the man.

Just then, the noise from the surrounding crowd began to increase. *The parade must be starting,* thought Josh, glancing around.

Sure enough, some people were strolling down the middle of the road. One man, in particular, was singing loudly and dancing like a clown. The people in the procession all appeared to be smiling and having fun. The boys tried to look for "gaps" in the crowd so that they could get a better look at what was happening...

"Isn't that the blind man?" queried Josh, when they finally managed to make their way closer to the front.

The old man with yellow pupils was now jumping for joy out in the middle of the crowd. HE was the "clown", and he kept hugging the man next to him. It was Rabboni. The blind man, though, called him by a different name: "Ee-ay-soos" or something like that.

Josh stared at the spectacle. He knew that only a few minutes ago, the old man had been blind. How could this same man now see and dance, without even using a walking stick, he thought, bewildered.

When Jacob, too, saw Rabboni, he realised what must have happened (although he was sorry that he hadn't seen him do it). Jacob was just about to explain the whole thing to Josh, when Rabboni stopped abruptly at the fig tree, just a few feet away from them. Rabboni then looked up and saw the mean guy sitting in the tree, and gestured for him to come down.

When the Tree Man eventually climbed out of the tree, Josh noticed that he was really quite short. *He doesn't look so high and mighty now,* Josh thought smugly.

Even though the Tree Man was dressed in expensive-looking clothes, he still looked really *sus*... Josh noticed that he didn't shake hands with Rabboni but remained close-fisted.

The crowd didn't seem to like the Tree Man either. Some people started to point their finger at him and laugh scornfully; others just cast him contemptible looks. It was clear that the Tree Man had "jipped" them in the past.

Rabboni, however, did not seem to care what people thought. Instead, he asked the Tree Man if they could "hang out" together. Jacob and the others looked on, horrified. They watched as the Rabboni and the short man wandered towards a luxurious-looking property, presumably the Tree Man's home.

The crowd could not understand why Rabboni (or anyone for that matter) would want to befriend such a awful, vile man. Their confusion, however, soon turned to rage…directed at Rabboni. Jacob started defending Rabboni, but no-one was listening to him.

"Why don't we head off?" asked Josh, pulling his friend away from the fickle crowd.

The boys moved a little further out, and stumbled upon a large pebble on the side of the road which they began to kick around. Within a short time, they were playing "soccer" with some of the local kids. They quickly forgot all about the Tree Man and Rabboni.

In fact, they were having such a good time, they almost missed the most amazing sight. The Tree Man had come out of his house and had begun calling out to all his neighbours. He then opened some heavy-looking sacks and began handing out money. A hoard of silver coins was being distributed to EVERYONE.

The Tree Man was laughing uncontrollably as he gave away his "dosh". This time, though, his laughter did not sound spiteful or malicious. The Tree Man actually sounded happy. Rabboni, too, looked pleased with his new friend, speaking words of encouragement to him.

Not surprisingly, people came rushing out from every direction, trying to grab as many coins as they could…

"C'MON! Let's get some too!" shouted Josh.

In the frenzy, Jacob and Josh even managed to spot some stray coins that had rolled between the crevices of the cobble-stoned roads. Very soon, the boys had acquired their own individual stash of shiny, new coins.

Josh carefully examined his collection, remarking: "This is TOTALLY AWESOME!"

He had never seen this type of money before – the coins had a Roman "head" on one side, and an Eagle on the other side. Buoyed by the day's success, the boys decided to return home.

CHAPTER 13: HIGH SPIRITS

Imma and Ally were in the throes of last-minute dinner preparations when the boys walked in the door. In fact, all the women in the entire courtyard seemed to be working at a more feverish pace.

When Ally spotted Josh, she began to whinge about all the extra cleaning and baking she had had to do that morning…and afternoon.

"You've got to be kidding me," she had told Imma earlier when she was shown the "proper" way of washing cups, pots, copper bowls, and even beds.

Josh, however, had his own stories to share about Rabboni and the Tree Man with the silver coins, so he tried to get a word in first. Imma, however, had other ideas. For the first time *ever*, she handed Josh a broom and indicated where she wanted him to sweep.

Jacob appeared to have gone up to the roof, probably to hide his money, concluded Josh. A short time later, Jacob reappeared smiling amiably, as he showed Imma one of his coins. Josh wondered where he had hidden the rest…

Shortly after, Av and Aaron also arrived home. The men put away their nets and equipment and cleaned themselves up, before they too presented themselves to Imma for work detail. *That's weird*, thought Josh, who had never really seen Av helping out in the house before.

Aaron and Jacob began to pull out a white tablecloth and place it over the chest table, while Imma produced two braided bread loaves, each with its own embroidered white cover. She then handed Ally two candlesticks (with long candles) to place on top of the table, and a jar of fragrant flowers.

I wonder if it's someone's birthday, Josh thought excitedly.

Av then pulled out a bottle of wine and one wine goblet, and stood before the table, proudly. Once the table was "set", the family members went upstairs to change their clothes. Each one later resurfaced, wearing clothes the children had not seen before.

When everyone had re-assembled and were about to start dinner, a dishevelled-looking stranger suddenly entered the room. He was warmly greeted by the family and was invited to join them. The children's curiosity was definitely piqued.

"It must be a party of some sort," Josh whispered to Ally, who stood next to him, watching with interest.

Then somewhere outside, they all heard what sounded like a horn being blown. In fact, six short horn blasts followed, and everyone stopped talking.

"What was that?" Brendan enquired of his siblings.

The family did not appear perturbed by the horn sound but immediately took their place at the table. The stranger also sat down, and everyone looked around with joyful anticipation. Jacob then dropped his new silver coin into a square box, which was sitting on the side of the table, before pushing the box towards the stranger. The stranger winked at him, appreciatively.

Imma then lit the two candles, shutting her eyes to shield them from the flames (presumably) while she said a prayer for her family. When she had finished, Av stood up and placed his hands on both Aaron's and Jacob's heads, and spoke loud words of affirmation. Both of his sons smiled enthusiastically up at their father. Av then moved towards Imma and began to praise *her* by reciting a rhyming poem. The gesture clearly meant a lot to Imma, who teared up a little before stroking Av's hand in a loving display.

Over the soft glow of candlelight, Av concluded with a final prayer, before allowing everyone to sample the wine, sharing the same cup. He did the same thing with the bread, handing out pieces to everyone around the table.

Once they had finished the bread and wine, the family started singing. Everyone was in high spirits, including the poor man whose toothless grin was on show all evening. Pretty soon, Brendan and Josh felt compelled to join in the refrain:

"Hahl-loo Ehl shah-dai!" they sang, over and over again.

Ally, however, felt embarrassed and did not join in. She did, however, help Imma serve the baked fish they had spent all day preparing. Ally felt a little proud of how she had stuffed it with delicious, ground whitefish.

The main course was then followed by a moist and creamy pudding, filled with nice crunchy noodles. After everyone had eaten and had enough, they sat back and relaxed, chatting away together. (Everyone was having a great time "chilling" and forgetting about the cares of the week.)

Two hours later, the stranger was finally farewelled and the family began preparing for bed. *What a strange dinner party,* Ally reflected. *No-one got drunk but everyone was really happy anyway.*

The next morning, after breakfast, the entire family walked towards the Village square. All the townspeople appeared to be heading towards the impressive-looking building with the large double doors. Today, it was open to the public, and a friendly doorman ushered them in.

The family walked straight into the main hall, which was supported by strong thick columns on three sides, and bench seating along two walls. Av and Imma quickly selected a place to sit down, and the children followed suit.

"What happens here?" asked Brendan in a loud voice, oblivious to the noise he was creating.

Ally whispered, "I think it's a community centre."

As she looked around, Ally suddenly recognised the angry mob seated near the front of the building. They had heard Brendan talking and were now glaring at the family, menacingly.

"OH MY GOD! What are they doing here?" Ally mouthed to Josh.

She automatically covered her entire head with her shawl, grappling awkwardly with the material in an attempt to hide her face. As Ally slumped down in her seat and lowered her gaze, Aaron observed the sudden change in her behaviour. His eyes were filled with concern. What could have caused Ally to look so frightened, Aaron wondered.

"I'm hungry," announced Brendan.

He had spotted some bread sitting on a serving plate, out the front of the Hall.

"Shhhh," whispered Ally, hoping Brendan would stop drawing attention to them.

Just then, Rabboni and his friends entered the building and took a seat. Brendan looked at Rabboni and exclaimed proudly: "Hey, I know him!"

Brendan immediately wanted to walk over to Rabboni and say "hello", but Imma held him close, and Brendan happily acquiesced, resting against her large stomach (which he thought felt very much like a big, comfortable pillow). His real Mum did not feel this soft. In fact, when Cassie held Brendan, all he could feel were sharp bones.

The leader out the front then invited Rabboni to read from a scroll. Rabboni stood up and faced the audience, before clearing his throat politely, and reading out loud. Everyone was listening intently, when all of a sudden, a man ran into the building, looked at Rabboni and shrieked.

"AAAAAAARGGGGGGGG!!!!" the man screeched, his entire body convulsing…

Brendan instantly buried his head in Imma's body. He was petrified.

The "psycho" then started screaming: "EESOUSS EESOUSS EESOUSS EESOUSS EESOUSS EESOUSS EESOUSS!!!"

When he then flung out his arms and bent his entire body towards Rabboni aggressively, everyone started running for cover. Av and Imma tried to steer the children out to safety but the exit was blocked by the sheer number of people pushing and shoving to get away. The children had no choice but to witness the entire frightening event. Brendan hid behind Imma's legs, and looked on in horror...

Rabboni then walked over to the "Psycho", and commanded him to STOP. With one word, the "evil spirit" began to shake the man hard, before giving a loud scream and coming out of him. Everyone was stunned.

The children's relief, however, was not shared by all… The blue tassels worn by the mob started jiggling as they raised their arms belligerently and began pointing at Rabboni. Rabboni, however, had started to walk back home, presumably to get his lunch.

CHAPTER 14: GONE FISHING

Soon after that, the family also sat down to lunch. However, the atmosphere was subdued, despite Av and Imma trying to lighten it up with more singing. Jacob kept asking his parents about Rabboni. His eyes were full of wonder and amazement at what he had seen. Brendan too wanted to talk about it.

"Who was that man who was yelling at Eesoos?" he quizzed his siblings.

"Who's Eesoos?" asked Josh, in between bites.

"You know Eesoos! He saved Ally from the angry men, and later, he took away my pain," Brendan retorted.

"Oh, you mean Rabboni," corrected Josh.

"No! His name is Eesoos," Brendan said indignantly. "That's what the crazy man called him."

Josh thought about what Brendan had said… *Was it possible that Rabboni had another name?*

After lunch, Av and Imma decided to go for a leisurely walk and Jacob and Brendan went with them. Brendan still looked a little anxious (presumably as a result of what he had seen earlier) and sought the reassurance of adult company. Aaron went upstairs to have a rest, not before looking at Ally to check if she was ok.

Both Ally and Josh remained seated at the table, as the others absconded. Josh tugged at Ally's arm, suggesting they "talk".

"K", she agreed.

"Listen, I have an idea," Josh said brightly. "I found some money yesterday, and I was thinking that we might have enough to buy a boat, so that the three of us could sail away from here."

"What are you talking about?" Ally asked disconcertedly.

Ally was physically and emotionally "spent" after everything she had endured over the last few days, and REALLY did not want to talk about stupid, childish fantasies.

"Well, I found some silver coins in the street. I figure, that if we have enough money, we could buy a boat... or pay someone to make us one. Either way, I think I could try to navigate our way back home by looking at the stars. I really think I could do it," Josh proposed.

"Josh, you're being stupid. First, you know nothing about sailing. God, you don't even know how to swim properly! Second, we don't have a boat, and no one's going to just give us a boat, are they? Third, what's Imma and Aar…" Ally stopped in mid-sentence. "What are they going to think about this?" Ally demanded.

Ally didn't know why she was about to speak his name out loud. He had barely spoken to her the whole time she had been here.

"I know I can't sail *yet*, but I could try to learn," Josh responded. "I was actually going to ask Av and Aaron if I can go out on their boat and see how they do it… And Ally, I've seen men chopping wood from the forest to build actual boats. There's even a blacksmith in the Village, shaping hot metal to make ship anchors and bolts. Don't you think we should, at least, try…?"

Josh desperately needed Ally's approval for this audacious plan. He looked at her pleadingly. Ally, however, just wanted to sleep. Over the last four days, she had been woken up before dawn and was extremely tired.

"Whatever," Ally said despondently and rolled her eyes. She just wanted to be left alone.

The next morning appeared to be a "regular" day. The weekend drama seemed to be over (at least for the adults). Brendan, however, had been crying in his sleep, and calling out for "Mummy"... He had clearly been having nightmares over what had occurred at the Community Centre. His crying had woken up Imma who had then taken him into her bed for the night. No-one had slept particularly well, but the morning beckoned.

First thing she knew, Ally had been seconded by Imma to grind some flour (for baking the day's bread) and was hard at it when Josh entered the kitchen. Ally looked flustered by the amount of energy needed to move the hand mill in continuous circular motions, but Imma sat alongside her, grinding the flour in tandem. Imma was also supervising Brendan who was playing at her feet, while giving "instruction" to Jacob.

"Shema Israel," Jacob enunciated in a loud voice. Then he began the prayer of "Shemone Esre..."

Josh, however, was determined to get busy with his plan of escape. After a small breakfast of warm bread and creamy cheese, washed down with a cup of frothy milk, Josh decided it was time to find Av and Aaron and learn how to sail. Brendan looked up from his toy, watching his brother gulp down his drink.

"Can I have some too?" he asked politely.

"Brendan, I don't have a lot of time. I'll pour you your own cup," Josh answered.

He understood Brendan's new-found addiction to fresh cow's milk. It tasted different to anything they had ever drunk at home. It was just like drinking melted vanilla ice-cream.

Leaving Brendan to form a milky "moustache", he farewelled Ally and the others and started off down the courtyard, despite the obvious look of disappointment on Jacob's face. Unlike Josh, Jacob still had his morning lesson to complete. (He knew that he would not be allowed to leave the house until it was done.)

Josh was not accustomed to being out on his own, and he looked around cautiously. The street looked "normal". There were a few veiled women carrying water jars above their heads, a donkey driver plodding along the street, and some children playing –one kid had a blindfold on and was trying to guess which of his friends had slapped him on the face. They were shrieking with laughter the whole time, until they spotted Josh. One of the kids called out to Josh, gesturing to him to join in, but Josh just shook his head, and the children quickly resumed their "guessing" game. Josh had important work to do today and did not have time to play games.

He continued along the rocky terrain in the direction of the lake, and passed several vineyards and fruit orchards along the way. These appeared to be flourishing in the subtropical climate. Josh spotted some large pomegranates, ripe for the taking. *Not today*, he told himself.

When he finally arrived at the lake, Josh began to look around for Av and Aaron. He quickly spotted them standing on their boat, using their oars to row out gently. There was a crew of three men working alongside them. Josh wondered who these men were. *Maybe the boat doesn't belong to Av... He and Aaron might actually work for someone else.*

"Oh man!" he said out loud.

If Av and Aaron were not in charge, they wouldn't be able to help him, Josh thought anxiously.

The men were not far from the shore. As he watched them, Josh noticed Aaron drop his oars and cast out a large, circular net. The net spread out and landed on the water like a giant parachute. It quickly descended, as it was laden down with thick ropes and metal weights. The men then sat down on the deck and chatted, occasionally peering over at the water.

Av noticed Josh sitting on the shore, and waved to him before inviting him to swim over towards them. Josh did not think that was such a good idea, as he didn't know how deep the water was and whether he could, in fact, swim that distance. Josh just shook his head in response, and decided to sit on the sand and wait for Av and Aaron to finish their work.

After a while, he saw Aaron and another guy from the boat, take off all their clothes, strip down to nothing, before diving down into the water. They both resurfaced clutching opposite ends of the weighted ropes, and together with the other men on board, they began to haul in their net. Seagulls circled above them, squawking in eager anticipation of a large catch… However, they were quickly disappointed when it became clear that only a few fish had been trapped beneath that giant net.

Not far from them, loud shouting could be heard. Av and the others looked in the direction of all the noise and saw another fishermen in a nearby vessel frantically signalling to them to come to his aid. He had managed to catch so many fish, his net was beginning to break.

Av and the others quickly rowed in the direction of this other boat, and pretty soon, both boats were so full of fish, they started sinking by the sheer weight of the haul. There were cries of absolute delight and panic at the same time.

Josh stood up to get a better look at the action. Between the fishermen's excited shouts, the turbulence of the waves created by the splashing of oars, not to mention the flock of seagulls flying dangerously close to the jerking fish, Josh could see Rabboni. He was just sitting quietly in the second boat. The fisherman who had signalled to Av was now bending down and kneeling. *Why is he bowing to Rabboni?* thought Josh, perplexed.

CHAPTER 15: REFLECTIONS

Josh realised that Av and Aaron would be busy for a while, disentangling the copious amounts of fish they had caught in their net. So he decided to go back to the house and wait for them there.

All the way back, he couldn't help thinking about what he had just seen. Rabboni appeared to be responsible for the huge haul of fish, but Josh couldn't work out HOW he had managed it. *Was he a fisherman... or a magician?* Josh was truly mystified.

One thing was certain. Rabboni *really* loved food. It seemed to Josh that he was usually feeding people, or eating with them.

When Josh got home, he looked around for Ally. Josh found her preparing dinner with the other ladies in the courtyard. Ally looked different to him... possibly a little older. She could have easily passed for one of the courtyard ladies.

"Ally, do you have a minute?" Josh asked shyly.

He hadn't really gotten to know the other women in the building, and didn't like interrupting them while they were talking. Ally looked over at Imma who nodded to her, indicating that it was ok to take a break. Ally and Josh then made their way outside. It was getting hotter as the day went on, but the light was certainly better outside. They found a shady spot on the stone steps just outside their building, and sat down.

"Hey, I tried to talk with Av and Aaron to ask them about the boat idea, but I couldn't get to them. I don't think the boat idea is going to work actually," Josh reported, matter-of-factly.

"What do you mean?" Ally interrupted.

"Well, I don't think Av owns his own boat. There were three other men with him, so I think he and Aaron might actually work for someone else –," Josh added.

"So?" she asked nonchalantly.

Ally was clearly not that impressed with the new information.

"Well, anyway. That's not all I wanted to tell you. While I was at the lake, I saw Rabboni again... or Eesoos. This time, though, he helped some fishermen catch so much fish, two boats almost capsized from the haul!"

"Well, maybe he knows something about fishing," Ally retorted. "Or he has the right gear, or bait, or whatever fishermen use," she added confidently.

Ally knew nothing about fishing – nor was she interested in talking about the "ins and outs" of fishing.

"No, you don't understand," Josh maintained. "Everyone was fishing in the same area. They all had the same nets, but the fish weren't biting for Av and Aaron, and then… two seconds later, all these fish landed in Rabboni's nets. It was SO cool!"

"What's the big deal?" Ally asked impatiently.

"Well, this man's incredible. That's what!" Josh replied petulantly.

He was actually a little annoyed that he couldn't impress Ally with this tale.

"Hey - what's wrong with you?" he queried.

Ally looked at him and hesitated for a moment, before muttering: "You wouldn't understand."

"I could try… if you tell me," replied Josh.

"OK, I'll tell you," Ally commenced. "I was putting some washing away for Imma, when…I saw myself."

"What do you mean?" Josh asked genuinely puzzled.

All he could work out was that Ally looked embarrassed.

"Well, Imma's got a mirror, like, in her chest. You can't see yourself really clearly, but come to think of it… I don't think I want to. I look hideous!" she suddenly blurted out.

"What do you mean? You look exactly the same as you've always looked, I swear!" Josh replied honestly.

"Thanks a lot. You're saying that I always look hideous."

"No…I didn't mean that. *You* know what I meant. Where's this mirror, anyway? Show it to me," Josh added, genuinely wanting to help.

Ally soon produced a circular object with an ornamental wooden handle, shaped like a female figure. The mirror's reflection was blurry and a little cloudy, as the "mirror" was actually polished metal, rather than glass. Ally held it up to her face, and was immediately repulsed by her reflection. She quickly thrust the object into Josh's hands.

"See! I told you… What am I going to do? My pimple crème is back home, and I don't have ANYTHING to put on my face. My skin's just going to get worse. I know it is!" Ally bemoaned.

Through the dim window, obscurely lit, stood Imma. She had been watching both Ally and Josh for a few minutes. She quickly went to her neighbour's fig tree, picked some ripened fruit, and came back into her kitchen, and began to peel away. She then pressed down the fruits' juicy red flesh into a bowl. Once that was done, Imma heated the mixture in the communal oven until it had become a nice, thick paste. Smiling contentedly to herself, she went to find Ally.

"What's this Imma? What are you making?" Ally asked, looking at the sticky brown mess.

Imma didn't answer her, but started applying her concoction to a soft gauze. Ally got up to leave, but Imma would have none of it, grabbing Ally by the hand, and forcing her to lay still. Imma's will finally prevailed and Ally stopped arguing with her. Imma then proceeded to cover Ally's entire face with the strange lotion.

"You look like an Egyptian mummy," chuckled Josh.

He wasn't exactly sure what was going on, but he knew Imma was trying to tend to Ally's blemished skin.

Once her face was fully coated, Ally sat very still and could feel her skin tightening as the medicine did its "thing" . It was actually kind of cool to have a facial, she thought. Ally had worked hard all morning and was feeling exhausted.

Ally also believed her period was due soon, which filled her with fresh anxieties about how she was going to manage it here... *Imma will know what to do,* Ally reflected, before shutting her eyes and taking a well-earned rest.

CHAPTER 16: JUST JAMMIN'

As it happened, the fig ointment worked masterfully on Ally's skin. The next morning, the red spots on her face had significantly reduced in size.   Ally's appearance was almost back to normal. Consequently, she was in a much better mood when Josh greeted her at breakfast.

"Good afternoon," she joked, when she saw him.

Everyone was already busy with their household activities when Josh sauntered in, sheepishly looking around the room. He did not like to be the last one up, but he was certainly not surprised to hear that Av and Aaron had left hours ago, taking breakfast with them to enjoy mid-morning.

Last night, on the roof, Josh had been racking his brains trying to think of another "escape plan". No matter how much he tried, though, the boat idea was the only one that made any sense.

"I'm going to try to find out about boats again," he informed Ally who was preoccupied with milling grain.

Josh noticed that she looked a lot more comfortable with the hand tool than she had yesterday.

Josh also tried to explain to Jacob that he was planning on going to the lakeshore. He didn't really mind if Jacob tagged along on this "mission". Jacob was a happy kind of kid, easy to get along with, and despite him not knowing English, the boys always managed to understand each other. Jacob grinned in agreement and went and gave Imma a kiss goodbye, before the two of them headed off.

Once outside, the boys could hear a lot of laughter coming from a group of the local children. When the kids saw Josh and Jacob, they called out to them excitedly and invited them to join in.

It looked to Josh like the kids were imitating a wedding ceremony. The "groom" wore a wreath of flowers on his head, almost like a crown, and was actually holding the hand of the "bride" who was dressed in a long, white gown. She wore a huge sash around her waist and a veil that hid her eyes (just like an adult lady). The bride also clutched a bouquet of flowers, while being slowly escorted down the street.

The regal-looking "couple" was preceded by some kids blowing flutes. *The tambourine players look really cool*, thought Josh. The "musicians" appeared to be having the most fun, as they jumped around the couple, dancing and beating their instruments boisterously. The "bridesmaids" followed closely behind the bride, carrying oil lamps, and singing joyfully as they accompanied the noisy procession.

Jacob started pulling at Josh's sleeve, inviting him to have a "go". Jacob clearly wanted to join in the play-acting. *I wouldn't mind beating the tambourine,* thought Josh.

Pretty soon, Josh was marching in formation down the street, enjoying the company of the other children and forgetting all about the lakeshore. Women from the Village started to peer down at the children from their upper floor windows. Surprisingly, none of the adults told them off for making so much noise.

Josh laughed as he watched Jacob dancing around like a crazy person, while trying to whack the other kid's tambourine. Everyone was having the best time. *As long as I don't have to be the "Groom," this game's pretty cool.*

Just as the kids rounded the corner of the street, something strange happened that changed their jovial mood… Without any warning, the "Bride" simply let go of the Groom's hand, her legs collapsing from under her, and she fell to the ground, her eyes rolling to the back of her head. All the children formed a tight circle around her, and stood there horrified. The bridesmaids gasped and covered their mouths in shock. No-one moved.

"Go get some help, QUICK!" Josh shouted to Jacob.

Jacob was woken from his reverie and ran off to find an adult. Josh began to rack his brains, trying to remember emergency first aid. *What are you meant to do, again?* he agonised.

Josh crouched down beside the girl and placed her on her side. (He was sure that this wouldn't hurt her). Josh then put his ear to her mouth to hear if she was breathing… He heard nothing.

"Hey, are you ok?" Josh yelled into the girl's ear.

She didn't respond, and Josh couldn't feel any breath…

"WAKE UP, WAKE UP!" he shouted, thinking he might be able to rouse the girl, if he yelled loudly enough...

"Hannah! Hannah!" the other kids called out, sensing the imminent danger.

Josh had no idea how to do CPR …and he knew he couldn't just ring for an Ambulance. He watched on helplessly, as the girl's limp, lifeless body just lay there. Then he saw blood trickling out of her nose.

Jacob eventually returned (completely out of breath) along with the leader of the Community Centre… the kind man who had ushered the family into the Temple. The man's expression was no longer happy or cheerful; he looked really scared. He quickly bent down to examine Hannah, before scooping her up in his arms and carrying her off in a frenzied rush.

Everyone seemed to know where the man was heading, and they followed closely behind him. *Perhaps there's a hospital or clinic somewhere nearby*, speculated Josh, as he tried to keep pace with the man.

When they arrived at a certain building, the man ran inside, still carrying Hannah in his arms. Everyone else just waited outside... (The building looked very much like a regular home.) A minute later, they could hear a woman crying, softly at first, and then sobbing loudly. Hannah's mother was mourning for her child and she could not be comforted.

"What's going on?" asked Josh.

All of the concerned neighbours then entered the house's courtyard, eager to help the family, but they were unable to *do* anything. The man then raced back out and began running towards the lake, this time, unencumbered by the weight of his daughter.

"Where's he going now? Where are the doctors? Isn't there anyone around who can help?" Josh queried Jacob.

Jacob just shrugged his shoulders and looked down at his sandals.

Everyone else hung around the house, and pretty soon, people started murmuring amongst themselves. As Josh studied the crowd, he noticed some of the kids were crying... Jacob too was tearing up.

"Has something happened? She's not *dead*... is she?" Josh began to panic.

Just then, Hannah's father returned with Rabboni. They were followed by a crowd of onlookers, eager to see what all the fuss was about.

Rabboni entered the property grounds, but motioned to the crowd to remain where they were…all except for three guys (presumably his closest friends) and, of course, Hannah's father.

When Rabboni walked through the courtyard and witnessed the chaotic scene, with women crying and wailing, he said something to the people gathered. They all just looked at him like he was crazy. Some even laughed, sarcastically.

Jacob grabbed Josh's hand and they stealthily made their way inside. (The boys needed to know what had happened to Hannah.) Rabboni and the adults appeared to have headed up to the sleeping quarters, so the boys followed.

They kept some distance behind the men, climbing only half way up the ladder, while trying to peer into their friend's bedroom. Only the top of the boys' heads were visible…

Sure enough, Hannah was lying motionless on her rose-coloured bed mat, surrounded by her Mother, her anguished Dad, Rabboni and his three friends. Rabboni then took Hannah's hand, and in a loud voice said:

"Talitha kumi!"

The lifeless Hannah suddenly opened her eyes, got up, and started walking around. She even spotted Jacob and Josh lurking in the stairwell, and waved to them. Everyone in the room turned around to see who she was waving at…

"Yipes," uttered Josh as he grabbed Jacob's arm before quickly scaling down the ladder. "I hope they didn't recognise us!" he called out to Jacob, as the boys raced towards the outer courtyard door.

The girl's mother then climbed down the ladder… only she wasn't looking for the boys. She walked straight into her kitchen, cut a piece of bread and put some orange jam on it…when she suddenly became aware of all the neighbours. They were clearly waiting for news of what had happened to Hannah.

Even though Hannah's Mum didn't actually speak to them, her expression said it all. She just stared at everyone, and started to laugh and cry at the same time. Hannah was going to be ok.

CHAPTER 17: THE ARTIFACT

"Wow! That was close..." Josh said with relief, as the boys quickly made their way through the crowd, and headed home.

Jacob was so pleased that Hannah was ok, he couldn't stop talking... presumably about the part Rabboni had played in the drama.

When the boys arrived home, they could see Brendan playing out the front of the house with a few of his friends. He was holding a strange-looking ball in his hands.

"What's that?" asked Josh, taking the ball away from him to examine it.

It appeared to be made of leather and filled with corn husks.

"Give it back!" insisted Brendan. Apparently, Brendan was teaching his friends how to play football.

Josh also spotted Ally and Imma around the side of the house, ankle deep in soil, gently beating out dill and cumin seeds with sticks. Ally looked happy to be outdoors with Imma, who was explaining the different types of vegetation in the garden.

When Ally saw Josh, she called out:

"Ciao! What's up?"

"Ally, you'll never guess what's happened. You really won't believe it… We just saw the most AWESOME thing EVER! We were just hangin' around when a girl dropped dead, right in front of our eyes!" Josh recounted, his eyes lighting up as he relived the incident.

"Shut up! Really?" exclaimed Ally, studying Josh closely to gauge if he was being serious. He looked fairly earnest.

"Are you for real?" Ally asked sceptically.

"Yeah! Hannah's her name… and she just stopped breathing. I'm 100 percent sure," Josh retorted.

"Imma, I gotta take a break," Ally called out as she slowly climbed out of the soil, and headed towards Josh.

Imma was just about to start threshing. The interruption, however, gave her an opportunity to speak with Jacob, and find out what had happened that day...

As Jacob, too, recounted every frightening detail for his Mother, Imma shook her head in disbelief, as she pondered how death had come in through the windows and entered the home of her neighbour, and cut down a child in the street. Imma queried why she hadn't been called to sing the appropriate funeral songs. Jacob told her that a call for mourners had apparently been made, but then abruptly cancelled.

"I should probably collect the laundry while you're talking," Ally told Josh, as she began walking indoors. "It should be dry by now. Come upstairs, and you can finish telling me the story there," she said.

Ally was carrying some leaves in one hand, when she noticed Josh staring at them.

"You could try some of these," she laughed. "Pistachio leaves are good for bad breath."

"*I* don't have bad breath," Josh responded, feeling a little hurt.

"Wanna bet?" she teased him. "Actually, all the adults here chew on these leaves. I figure that since we don't have any Colgate, WE should probably try some too."

When they got to the roof, Ally put the leaves down, while she busied herself collecting the washed linen and folding the items separately. Josh continued on with his story:

"So - Rabboni then got called to this girl's house. He went upstairs with her parents, to where she was lying, and he spoke some words to her. And that's all it took… She just got up."

"I dunno, Josh. It sounds a little bogus," quipped Ally. "I mean, if she was really dead, she was dead –right? Perhaps, she only fainted or something…"

"No, Ally. It really happened. I saw it with my own eyes! Rabboni's amazing. I know he looks fairly 'ordinary'… but I swear, he can do the most awesome things!" Josh protested.

But Ally had stopped listening. She was staring intently at something on the roof. Next to the fishing equipment, the sun had illuminated something that was partly hidden by the netting. When Josh also looked down, he noticed a hard slab of flint with a chalk drawing on it. Ally picked it up to take a closer look. Imprinted on the smooth face of the stone, was a picture of a beautiful woman. The two of them stared at it for the longest time.

The artist had captured the woman's alluring stare and her deep honey-coloured eyes, which were softened with tiny yellow specks.

"Hey, that looks exactly like YOU.
Who drew this?" Josh asked.

Ally quickly placed the stone drawing back in the same position as where she had found it. She didn't answer Josh.

CHAPTER 18: THE BETROYAL

That night over dinner, Ally was too embarrassed to look at Aaron. She managed to help serve the family meal and chew her food without meeting his steady glance. As most of the dinner conversation usually took place between the male members of the household, Av and the boys did not notice anything different. But Aaron did. He couldn't understand why Ally was acting so *distant*. He deliberately brushed his fingers along the serving plate of vegetables she held out to him, forcing her to acknowledge him, but to no avail. Ally simply ignored him.

The truth was that Ally was scared to look into his eyes, afraid that she would learn how deeply he felt about her. Over the course of the evening, she tried to keep busy, helping Brendan with his food, and rearranging the bowls on the table… but she knew that she would have to face Aaron eventually.

What should I do? What should I say?? Ally worried. She had no idea how to talk to any guy, let alone, Aaron… this attractive, OLDER man… who didn't understand English.

Aaron's penetrating glance finally paid off.

Ally stole a quick look at him, and then she couldn't look away. His eyes lit up and drew her in.

Imma stared at both of them and her face clouded over. Something was troubling her, and she knew she had to talk to Av about it.

Ally, however, could scarcely contain her excitement. When it was time for bed, she was completely preoccupied - it took ages before sleep would come...

The next morning, Imma was the same loving and kind person towards Ally, but slightly more serious. Later on that day, when everyone had finished dinner, she "shoo-ed" Ally and the boys away, leaving her and Av alone with Aaron.

"What's going on?" Josh enquired of Jacob.

"Ketubah," replied Jacob authoritatively.

"What's that?"

Jacob just shrugged his shoulders at him, and quickly pulled out the checkers game.

Ally, however was intrigued by the adults' covert behaviour. She could sense that Aaron was uncomfortable. He said something to his parents, before slowly getting to his feet, and following them outside. (Aaron was clearly not happy to be going out, and walked a few paces behind his parents.)

When the three of them exited the house carrying oil lamps, Ally made a quick decision to follow them. The younger boys were distracted with their game and didn't even see her leave.

It's SO COLD, now that it's dark… Ally's teeth were chattering as she kept her eyes pealed. She quickly spotted the three figures carrying lit lamps. As Ally had no lamp of her own, she had to tread carefully, for fear of tripping over the roughly strewn pavement…but at least, *they* would not see her.

Av, Imma and Aaron finally stopped outside a neighbouring house and knocked loudly on the wooden door. Amid the darkness and the night dew, Ally could hear Av's voice identifying himself, before the door was quickly opened and all three were warmly embraced and welcomed inside.

I wonder who lives there, thought Ally. From the shadows where she stood, Ally could see directly into the front room. She remained very still, trying to work out what was happening inside… Ally could see Aaron and his parents being invited to recline at the family table. The adults were soon joined by a girl, around Ally's age. *Surely they're not going to eat again?*

The woman of the house then placed a jug of wine with goblets before her guests... Ally ventured closer to the window. *If only I could understand what they're saying,* she thought dejectedly.

Ally then noticed Av pulling out a document from under his cloak. He passed it to Aaron who tentatively handed it to the girl, who smiled coyly, before passing it on... The document was examined by the man, who beamed with pride and nodded his head in agreement. Av then poured a cup of wine and handed it to his son. Aaron, however, did not drink the wine but sat motionless, until his father gave him a sharp nudge. With his Dad's prompting, Aaron finally offered the cup of wine to the smiling girl, who accepted it from him, and eagerly downed its contents.

Both sets of parents then clapped their hands, as if celebrating, and then hugged Aaron and the girl. Imma even produced some gifts that had been concealed in her coat pockets...clearly intended for the girl. The girl was thrilled to receive the various gifts (which appeared to be mostly shiny jewellery) and gushed her appreciation in Aaron's direction.

As Ally watched in dismay, tears began to form in her eyes. She tried hard *not* to cry. Discouraged and confused, Ally ran back to the house and got into her bed. Before she knew it, tears were streaming down her cheeks.

CHAPTER 19: BEST MATES

The next morning, Ally went about her normal chores, milking the cow, and fetching the family's water before breakfast. She found some comfort in the simple, structured routine that had become her "life" over these past two weeks. It actually helped dull the pain of last night.

Ally started thinking about everything that had happened in the Village. On the one hand, it seemed weird to her that Av and Imma would take in three strangers, like her and the boys. Then again, Ally had noticed lots of travellers being "hosted" by the villagers. The people here were generally kind. However, when it was all said and done, the children had been looking for peace…but nothing really good had happened to them…they had hoped for healing, but terror had come instead.

Josh's thoughts were firmly fixed on Rabboni and the incredible things that he had seen him do. He waited until after breakfast, before grabbing Jacob's arm and ushering him out the door:

"Let's go find Rabboni," he said brightly.

Jacob smiled knowingly, and the two boys set off on their quest. It appeared that they weren't the only ones with the same idea. The news about Rabboni had spread so widely that huge crowds of people were out looking for him… There were even people who *Jacob* did not recognise, scouring the Village searching for Rabboni.

The strangers were dressed more impressively than everyone else, with unusual scripts pinned to their foreheads and arms, and huge tassels for everyone to see. (The writing reminded Josh of the Arabic typesetting font on his laptop at home). Josh thought that these men strutted around the Village like they *owned* it.

"What show-offs," he whispered to Jacob when they were out of earshot.

Josh noticed that these men enjoyed being greeted by all the locals. Old folk were even prepared to give up their own seats, so that the strangers could sit down. The strangers accepted the seats, not giving a second thought to the elderly men who now had to stand.

Passers-by were addressing the strangers with the name, "Rabboni." *I guess there could be a few people with the same name*, deduced Josh.

Josh, however, was only interested in ONE Rabboni. He didn't like the look of these other guys, especially when he saw them conferring with the angry mob who the children had met on their first day.

"Let's get away from here," he motioned to Jacob.

The boys continued walking until they came to a house which was surrounded by heaps of people. Suspecting that Rabboni might be inside the home, the boys tried to make their way in, but they couldn't even reach the front door. (There were *so* many people blocking their way.) Just then four men arrived, carrying a guy on a stretcher.

"Hey, I know that man," exclaimed Josh. "He fell down the steps at the Community Centre. It was awful. He fell right on top of Brendan… there was blood everywhere!"

The injured man's eyes were half open and his breathing was laboured. Josh watched as his four friends attempted to carry him inside the house. *Poor man,* thought Josh. He appeared to be in a great deal of pain.

"Too bad they can't get to Rabboni," he told Jacob. "He would definitely be able to fix him."

The boys watched as the men gently put the stretcher down to catch their breath. They wiped their sweaty hands on their tunics, as they talked about what to do… One of them suddenly began to point to the house. With renewed energy, each man picked up their end of the stretcher and headed back towards the house, but this time, they veered to the right, and began climbing the outside staircase.

Why are they going up to the roof? Josh thought, scratching his head.

"Let's follow them, and see what they're up to," he told Jacob.

When the boys climbed up the staircase, they saw the men actually cutting up a section of the roof. The roof was thatched, but still very strong, as it was supported by wood beams and reeds, bound together with a thick mud mortar. After a great deal of effort, the men managed to make a sizeable hole in the roof. And with that…they carefully lowered the stretcher down into the middle of the house.

A man from inside the room started yelling at them and pointing at his torn roof (and the furniture which was now covered in cascading mud, straw, and reeds). The boys crept up closer to get a better look. Rabboni was definitely downstairs… but he wasn't concerned about the roof, or the mess. He was talking quietly to the injured man.

Why doesn't Rabboni DO something? Josh wondered as he tried to understand what was happening downstairs. Josh could only see the top of Rabboni's head and the sick man, lying stiffly across the stretcher.

The man's friends were still crouched on the roof, looking down at Rabboni expectantly. But then, almost like Rabboni was reading everyone's thoughts, he motioned for the sick man to stand up. And the man did. He immediately got to his feet, straightened up, picked up his mat and started walking towards the front door. His friends raced towards the staircase to meet him, almost tripping over the boys in their haste.

When the men saw their mate bounding over the gate, they all cheered and clapped. Eventually, the five of them decided to make their way home...but were constantly stopped by passers-by, eager to learn what miraculous thing had happened in the house.

Josh just gaped, completely amazed. Jacob, however, lifted his eyes skywards. His face was full of fear as he uttered words of thanks...

CHAPTER 20: BED BUGS

Ally woke up feeling sick. She suddenly realised that her period had arrived during the night. When she looked down at the bedding, her worst fears were confirmed:

"Kill me now!" she announced aloud, when she saw blood stains all over her bed mat.

Noticing her absence and hearing the commotion upstairs, Imma popped her head up the ladder and quickly surmised what must have happened. She gestured to Ally to remain in bed… so Ally waited for Imma to come to her aid.

Finally, a bandage made out of a type of green moss was produced – this took a while as it was fossicked from the garden. Imma then fastened it to a brown woollen cord to keep it in place, which passed up to another cord around the hip region.

During her "fitting", Ally tried to hide her obvious humiliation. *What I would give for my Tampax right now…* she cringed silently. This process was excruciatingly long.

Imma then changed Ally's bed mat with a fresh one, and helped Ally back into bed. The new rolled-out mat was scented with fragrant cinnamon. *Hopefully, it will cover up the smell,* Ally thought miserably… She hadn't washed in a while and was convinced that she stunk.

"Thanks Imma," she muttered.

Ally was not used to having anyone care for her so tenderly (especially with her period). Imma worked both lovingly and efficiently, sensitive to the heightened sense of embarrassment experienced by the "patient".

Ally had gotten her period before but had learned to "muddle" her way through by watching various *YouTube* clips and asking some of her closest friends what to do. Her Science teacher had also explained "the basics" to the girls. She had recommended using sanitary pads "so you could see what was coming out." Ally had since experimented with tampons.

"I feel really sick in the tummy," she complained to Imma, who looked on sympathetically, as she stroked Ally's forehead.

Imma then went downstairs to make a hot herbal tea for Ally to sip. It smelt mostly of liquorice and parsley, and it was sweetened with honey.

"Thanks Imma," said Ally.

Even though it didn't smell particularly good, Ally trusted Imma's medicinal knowledge.

With no *Mylanta* on hand, Ally drunk her tea and willed herself to feel better. She then slept a little.

When she woke, Ally realised that some time had passed. Imma must have visited while she was sleeping, as Ally noticed a new moss-stuffed napkin sitting nearby, ready to be used by the "patient".

Ally picked it up and examined it. It felt very much like a fine sponge. The first bandage, however, seemed to be doing the job…when she checked, nothing had escaped during her sleep. *Awesome!* Ally thought. Her stomach was feeling much better too.

Ally decided to get up and see what was happening downstairs.

"Hi Imma," she said when she spotted Imma preparing to wash her bed mat.

Imma looked up at her, mortified.

"Shush!" Imma said and quickly ushered Ally back to bed, apparently scandalised to see her downstairs. Somewhat reluctantly, Ally did as she was told.

How weird, Ally thought perplexed… Imma looked almost frightened to see her.

Ally then slept a little more. When she woke up, she could hear that the men had returned home from work. Ally was feeling pretty isolated upstairs, so she decided to get out of bed, change her bandage, and venture downstairs. However, before she could even enter the living area, Imma yelled at her, and gestured that she should get back up. Rebuffed again, Ally returned to bed. She didn't like being physically separated from the rest of the family.

Back home, Ally couldn't wait to go to her room, and shut out the rest of the family. Here, though, things were different. *She* was different, Ally suddenly realised.

Ally wondered how Josh and Brendan had spent their day. Josh was probably thinking of "escape plans", she smiled to herself. Brendan, on the other hand, appeared to have adjusted quite well to life here. He was even sleeping through the night, without having nightmares or "accidents" (unlike her).

Suddenly, Ally heard someone coming up the ladder. *OMG!* she thought. *It's Aaron.*

Aaron subsequently entered the room a little hesitantly, and just stood there, looking at her... Ally was shocked to see him, and tried to explain what she was still doing in bed:

"I woke up sick today...but I'm actually feeling ok now."

Aaron gazed into her eyes and tried to say something. They seemed to have a connection that went beyond words.

Ally was still upset about what she had witnessed the other night, and Aaron seemed to have picked up on her "cues". He sat down at the foot of her bed mat and produced a yellow flower from his cloak. As Aaron handed it to her, his eyes never left hers.

"That's so pretty," Ally said shyly, taking it from him and holding it close enough to examine its petals.

Ally so wished she had her iPhone to find some words that he might understand. She was sure that she was blushing and Aaron would be able to see her colour rising. (Part of Ally even wished Aaron would leave the room now...) Ally's heart was beating so quickly, and she had a strange feeling in the pit of her stomach - different to period pain, but equally uncomfortable.

Aaron picked up Ally's oval-shaped pendant which was lying on the floor, next to her mat. He fingered the domed glass over the intricate design, studying the image contained within. The background was blue glass, representing surrounding waters and it had a fine gold-coiled wire, weaving around the map of Australia.

Just then, Imma walked in and saw them both.

"Nephaq!" she reproached Aaron, and he quickly got to his feet. He offered some words of explanation to his Mum, before hastily exiting the room. Ally had no idea what he said but she realised (at that moment) that she trusted Aaron.

Imma then followed Aaron downstairs. Ally strained her ears to hear what they were discussing, but all she could understand was the word "mikva". Mikva was the bath… she knew that much. Why would Imma insist that Aaron now wash in the mikva? Ally was confused. *Imma's acting like I have bugs or something… Surely she doesn't think that I could infect anyone?*

CHAPTER 21: THE SPITTING IMAGE

Josh was also ushered away from Ally's room when he had ventured upstairs. Believing her to be too sick to receive visitors, he decided to stay away from the house and accompany Jacob to the Community Centre instead.

Lots of kids had already gathered at the Centre, which seemed to "double" for a School. When class commenced, Jacob was asked by the Community Leader to read from the special scrolls that were stored there. It appeared that Jacob already knew how to read and write fairly well… but at the Community Centre, he was getting taught the "harder" stuff. The other students waited eagerly for their turn to read as well.

OK, so the Centre's like a school for older boys, concluded Josh. Strangely, though, all the kids at this school were very well-behaved and were listening attentively – there were no "bad" kids at all in this class, Josh noticed.

It turned out that Hannah's Dad was the Teacher. He gently instructed his male pupils throughout the day and taught them patiently. Josh couldn't help thinking back to the day when

Hannah had died, and the anguish he had seen on her Dad's face. Today, he looked vastly different. He was even cracking jokes with the boys, Josh observed with delight.

The only textbook the boys used was a scroll with wooden handles, called the "Tenakh". When their Teacher referred to the "Tenakh", it sounded like he was clearing his throat and getting ready to spit. The boys handled it with the utmost care, like it was *very* important. Josh was interested in the readings for a little while, but then his thoughts drifted to Ally. He wondered what was wrong with her…

After "school" the kids decided to play marbles in the street instead of going straight home. *That looks fun*, Josh mused, when he saw some children digging a straight row of holes in the ground. Each kid then took turns to roll their "marbles" into the holes, from about six feet away. Some kids even tried to toss them instead of rolling them. Both methods were within the rules, Josh learned.

"Hey, what are these made of?" Josh quizzed Jacob, picking up one of the odd-looking "marbles".

Jacob laughed as he ran towards a flock of sheep grazing nearby. He grabbed one sheep from behind and tried to hug its white and brown neck. Its ears were long and drooping and it was looking at Jacob with serious consternation. The sheep was fairly tame, but when Jacob tried to lift one of its feet, to show Josh, the sheep was having none of it and scampered away.

"What are you doing?" Josh asked him.

Was Jacob trying to tell him that the marbles were really bone joints… from a sheep's foot? Josh was bewildered by this, but tried to forget about what he was actually holding, and concentrate on scoring points.

Later that day, when Josh arrived home, he went to visit Ally but was thwarted by Imma (once again). Imma was adamant that Ally remain on her own. *She must really be sick,* thought Josh.

"Hopefully, she'll be better tomorrow?" he enquired of Imma, who responded with a smile…

At a bit of a loose end, the boys decided to head out again. They ended up exploring in the nearby hills. *We're sure to have another adventure,* thought Josh with great anticipation.

Josh was NOT really keen on climbing, but apparently, Jacob had something special he wanted to show him… something he had recently discovered... so Josh shadowed him up the mountainous terrain, and soon they were both standing in front of a large opening in the mountain.

"Seriously? Is this an actual cave?" Josh's eyes widened.

Jacob had clearly been here before and ventured in without hesitation. Josh decided to stick close behind him. Beyond the narrow entrance, the cave sloped down into a vast dark chamber.

"What was that?!" Josh jumped with fright when some drops of water trickled down from the cave's roof. Jacob laughed good-naturedly. He then showed Josh the cave walls which were full of graffiti.

"Hey, these are really cool," said Josh trying to make sense of the images engraved on the stonework. He could see figures of people and animals quite clearly.

Beyond the chamber, lay several tunnels along shadowy pathways. The boys' exploration was cut short though, when they heard some loud voices coming from the entrance to the cave…

"Someone's coming," whispered Josh. "Quickly…hide!"

The boys scrambled to find a place to conceal themselves. They crouched down in the back of the darkened cave and waited quietly. From the cover of darkness, they saw two men standing at the entrance but they could not make out their faces, as the light behind them was creating a lot of glare. One man was making strange sounds and tapping his hand on the surrounding rock.

I wonder if he's deaf…or just really dumb? Josh thought.

The boys then watched as the other man put his fingers in the dumb man's ears. He then spat on his (own) fingers before touching the dumb man's tongue. As he did this, he looked upwards, sighed deeply, and said:

"Effatha!"

That's so gross, squirmed Josh.

The dumb man then started to talk… really clearly. It was like his ears had been opened, and his twisted tongue had been released. Keen to demonstrate his extraordinary new speaking skills, the man even started to sing out loud!

All because of some spit, marvelled Josh.

CHAPTER 22: REVELATIONS

When both men finally left, the boys hurried out of their hiding spot. Jacob couldn't contain his excitement, and kept repeating:

"Eesoos! Eesoos!"

Josh hadn't seen Rabboni's face. Could it really have been Rabboni? Josh mulled it over in his head. It was the kind of thing that Rabboni *would* do, he thought. This time, however, there were no massive crowds to witness the amazing feat.

Later that night, Josh tossed and turned on his bed mat. He kept thinking about Rabboni. *Who is this man?* Josh asked himself. *And how can he do all these things? Was it magic or something else?*

The only magic tricks Josh had ever seen involved a deck of cards… He had also watched TV shows featuring "illusionists" who performed all sorts of clever acts.

Rabboni was different though, Josh believed. He used his power to HELP people. Also, Rabboni wasn't interested in getting people's applause. Like in the cave… there was no-one around to SEE him fix that man's speech. Rabboni never even raised his voice, like the illusionists did. (You always knew when they were about to do a death-defying act… they usually "prepared" their audience to witness something amazing.) Rabboni, though, was not a show-off. Also, the things Josh had seen Rabboni do, looked REAL. They couldn't just be "illusions", could they? Josh suddenly became very confused. *Do these things happen IRL (in real life) or not?* he wondered.

The Village was real. Josh was sure of that. The people who lived here were real too. He had lived amongst them now for almost two weeks. He knew them really well. Sure, they were different… To start with, they were foreigners speaking some strange-sounding language. But they had taught him lots of things… and he liked them. Also, Josh reasoned that the whole two weeks couldn't be a dream. (He had never experienced a dream that had lasted that long.) And yet, he still couldn't explain all the amazing things he had seen.

Josh wished Ally could have been with him the entire time, and witnessed everything he had seen. He decided to go and speak to Ally, even though it was the middle of the night.

Josh quietly crept out of his bed and climbed down the ladder to her room.

"Hey, are you awake?" he whispered in Ally's ear.

"What's wrong? Is it morning?" she murmured, jolted by this nocturnal visit.

"No, but I have to talk to you," Josh urged.

"Ok…let's go downstairs," Ally said sluggishly.

She brushed aside her drowsiness and followed Josh down the ladder. They went and sat in the open courtyard, empty now from the chatter and activities of the day. The oven hearth was still flickering small embers, providing orange light, and a little warmth.

"So, what's so important you had to wake me up?" Ally asked conspiratorially.

She knew it must be serious. Josh wouldn't normally do anything that thoughtless, she reasoned. He had her full attention.

"I really wanted to talk to you over the last few days, but I haven't seen you at all," Josh explained apologetically.

"I know…" Ally agreed. "Imma's treating me like a prisoner. I've got my period, but it's like, I'm infected or something."

"What do you mean?" Josh asked, raising one eyebrow.

"It's like Imma doesn't want me to go outside or talk to anyone… just because I've got my period. Can you believe that?" Ally uttered in disbelief. "And she washes everything I touch…my bed mat, my clothes, her clothes, everything! It's crazy."

"Well... I've been looking for a way out of this place. And I finally think I've found it." Josh changed the subject to something he felt more comfortable discussing.

"Are we still talking about the boat idea…coz I've got to tell you, Josh, I can't see that happening," Ally pronounced with equal resolve.

Ally didn't like the thought of sailing off with two "kids". For starters, she knew Josh was not a good swimmer. Then, there was the whole question of *where the hell they were,* to consider.

"Rabboni's our way out of here," Josh suddenly declared.

"What do you mean?" Ally asked sceptically.

Ally knew Rabboni had been good to them, but she could not understand how one man could possibly get them out of this mess…

"OK, listen," Josh began. "I've watched this guy, and he can do things no-one else can do… like, AMAZING things."

"Yasss, I know what you've told me," Ally stifled a yawn. "But I'm still not sure how he can help *us*."

"Damn it, Ally. You're not really listening," Josh said exasperatedly. "I've seen a man who couldn't walk, suddenly leaping around like a deer… the eyes of a blind man opened, and a guy who couldn't speak, suddenly talking properly and even singing. Not to mention, a dead girl being raised back to life! YOU even saw Rabboni forcing out evil spirits…with just one word. He's really powerful, Ally. He can do ANYTHING. All we need to do is tell him what's happened to us and ask for his help. HE will sort out the rest!" Josh's face was flushed with excitement.

Ally stared at Josh. He looked completely fairdinkum. It was true that Rabboni had done some cool things, but did he really have supernatural powers? Ally was doubtful.

"Let me think about it, Josh. I'm *really* tired. Can we go back to bed now?"

Ally got to her feet without waiting for Josh to respond. It was way too late to decide anything tonight, she thought.

CHAPTER 23: DREAMTIME

Lying back on his mat, Josh looked up at the sky. The open roof revealed a striking moon and a galaxy of shining stars, all in their proper place. Josh reckoned that the Bear and Orion were present, and started thinking about the Pleiades and the other constellations in the southern sky.

Josh wondered if God brought them all out like an army, one after another, calling each by its name… Surely, he thought, if God could create the universe, and command the sun to give light to the day, and the moon and stars to shine at night, then anything was possible…Perhaps God had also sent Rabboni to rescue them?

Josh started to feel more relaxed about the future. In time, he drifted off to sleep.

Ally, on the other hand, started to think about everything that Josh had said, and found it exceptionally hard to get back to sleep… She tossed and turned for ages, and when she finally drifted off, she had the weirdest dream. She was talking to Rabboni, but it wasn't really *Rabboni.*

The man in her dream was dressed in a long robe and he wore a golden sash around his chest. The hair on his head was white like wool (as white as snow) and his eyes were like blazing fire… His feet were also glowing like bronze being heated in a furnace, and his voice sounded like the roar of a waterfall. And he spoke directly to her:

"Ally, don't be afraid," he said reassuringly. "Someday I will bring you home from foreign lands. You and your family will live in peace and safety, with nothing to fear. So don't be afraid!"

Ally felt strangely comforted by this encounter with the weird-looking Rabboni. Even though she was still sleeping, she felt a heavy weight being lifted off her shoulders, and she slept soundly until morning.

The next day, Imma started checking Ally's bed mat with a great deal of interest. After a detailed inspection, Imma decided it was now "safe" for Ally to resume normal work activities…and she ushered Ally into the mikveh for a proper wash.

"Yay!" Ally quietly cheered, realising that her period was finally OVER…

After taking an unusually long bath (it was the first one she had taken in a while) it appeared that it was time for Ally to participate again in all the family activities…or "Melachah" as Imma called it (which Ally knew meant *work*).

While she had really missed her Tampax, Ally thought the worst thing about getting her period had been being cooped up for so long. She really craved some natural sunlight. It was so dark indoors…

Ally was also surprised to learn that she missed seeing people and hearing their conversations. Even though she didn't understand everything that the courtyard women chatted about, Ally did miss being amongst them. She had no phone, or books, or anything interesting to *do* on her own.

Ally suddenly realised that the courtyard ladies didn't really need to *Snapchat* or text anyone, as their friends were always around. *It's pretty cool, when you think about it…* Ally smiled.

She began to grind the grain needed to bake the day's bread, working happily alongside her "nearby friends". The ladies had clearly missed her too, and expressed as much with hugs, huge grins, and endless chatter. When Ally went to fetch water from the local well, she felt positively "normal" again.

In this Village, there was a time to dream and a time to grind. For Ally, the time for dreaming was fortunately over.

CHAPTER 24: TRIPPING AROUND

Josh thought there was no time to lose in his quest to find Rabboni. He decided that the lake was a good place to start his search, as he had often seen Rabboni hanging around with fishermen. It occurred to him that these particular fishermen might actually live near the lake. Perhaps, too, Rabboni was staying at someone's house down there, Josh thought excitedly.

Jacob was being "home-schooled" that morning, with Ally and Brendan observing at a distance. It was probably better that Jacob wasn't able to go out, concluded Josh, as he would have only distracted him from his mission… and Josh couldn't afford to waste another second.

After breakfasting on chickpeas with pita bread, and spiced yoghurt washed down with a cup of pomegranate juice, Josh said goodbye to the others, and ventured out into the warm sun. The juice tasted both tangy and sweet, as he licked the last remaining residue off his lips.

There appeared to be fewer people around today. Keeping the ravine to one side of him and the mountain rise on the other, Josh walked along the path, overtaking various townspeople. They paid no particular notice of Josh as he steadily made his way down towards the lake.

Adjacent to the lake shore, Josh noticed a type of fish factory, where dealers of fish were busy salting and pickling the day's catch. *I've never eaten so much fish in my whole entire life*, Josh thought. Most of the fish was really well seasoned with salt and various other herbs, and it always tasted delicious.

Josh's family in Melbourne were mainly meat eaters, beef and lamb mostly. He suddenly realised that he hadn't missed eating meat while he had been living in the Village.

Squinting at the boats on the water, he could see Aaron and Av out on their fishing vessel, but the men next to them looked different. A fresh team had evidently been assigned to help Av and Aaron.

The men who had been hangin' with Rabboni were nowhere to be seen…so Josh decided to search for the fishermen's homes instead. He spotted some large properties nearby, and went to investigate.

These fishermen must be richer than Jacob's family, thought Josh as he observed the larger size of the stone structures. He saw some kids playing marbles on the road nearby, and decided to find out if they knew anything.

"Is Rabboni near here?" he asked hesitatingly, not sure whether the children would understand him.

Puzzled for a moment, the children looked at one another, before finally shaking their heads and pointing southerly, whilst repeating a strange word – presumably, the name of a place. (Josh had never heard of it before.)

"Thanks," Josh replied dejectedly.

It was clear that Rabboni was not around the lake anymore. More importantly, it suddenly dawned on Josh that he had no idea *where* Rabboni came from…or if he would even be coming back here.

Crestfallen, Josh began to walk back along the path, kicking the boulders and pebbles underfoot, while he considered his next move. He began to think that perhaps Jacob might prove useful to him in his search for Rabboni. At least, Jacob would be able to understand the place the children had mentioned, and perhaps, lead Josh directly to Rabboni…so he headed back home, to enlist Jacob for this vital mission.

Jacob was outside when Josh neared the house, and greeted his friend enthusiastically. He was really excited to see him back. The boys started exchanging their news simultaneously. Jacob spoke of his plans for the two of them, while Josh talked about trying to locate Rabboni.

When Jacob finally caught his breath long enough to *listen* to Josh, he slapped the side of his head good-naturedly and exclaimed "Yerushalayim," over and over again.

"What? Yeru-shala-yim? Is that where Rabboni is staying? Can we go there? How long will it take us?" Josh hurled heaps of questions at him.

Sensing Josh's urgency, Jacob ran inside to ask Imma about travelling to "Yerushalayim". He found her concentrating hard on separating threads, a time-consuming but important task in weaving wool. Imma was pleased to see her son looking so happy. Not wanting to quash his spirit, Imma began to discuss the issue with the courtyard women. Between them, it was quickly discovered that another family was planning to travel to the same town, providing the perfect opportunity for the boys to tag along.

Arrangements were then put in place for Josh and Jacob to accompany Imma's friends to Yerushalayim. And judging from the amount of food Imma packed for them, and her inclusion of rolled bed mats, Josh understood that the trip would require an overnight stay.

Excited by the prospect of finding Rabboni, Josh and Jacob helped load up the family's donkey, who let out a loud call as more and more gear was being packed and tied to his back. He was usually an even-tempered animal, and very domesticated, but he knew that today he was a "working" animal, and not a family pet. (This was despite the fact that Av kept him stabled indoors overnight, just beneath the family's sleeping quarters.)

With the packing mostly completed, Josh went to find Ally.

"Hey, Ally- Jacob and I are going to find Rabboni. But the thing is, he's staying in another town, so we have to go away for a few days so we can properly look for him," Josh explained.

"What are you going 'on' about?" Ally looked up while she washed the wool Imma had handed her.

"We have to travel to another town called Yerushalayim, to find Rabboni…so we'll be gone for a few days," Josh repeated.

"Are you serious?" Ally stopped her work and just stared at him.

"This trip is our only chance, Ally…"

It was nearing the time to leave. Josh had never hugged Ally before, and it felt weird to start now. So he didn't. Instead, he just said good-bye to her and smiled, and then went to find Brendan, who barely looked up from his game. Brendan was enjoying a serious contest with the neighbourhood kids involving toy soldiers, when he felt his older brother patting him on the head, and hearing a promise to "see him in a couple of days." Brendan didn't even see Josh leaving.

With the "good-byes" effectively said, it was time for the boys to commence their road-trip.

CHAPTER 25: CAT-ASTROPHE!

Sure-footed and eager to reach their destination, Josh and Jacob ran ahead of the group, leaving their donkey to be guided by the adults. The convoy consisted of two main families with children of varying ages, parents, grandparents, and of course, "acquaintances" like Jacob and Josh. They were a largish group, but happy to be travelling together, and there was a lot of friendly banter between the adults, not to mention the excitable chatter by the younger members of the group. No-one seemed perturbed by the added responsibility of the two extra charges.

There was no close supervision of the children – they skylarked and ambled along at their own pace without anyone telling them to *behave themselves*. Josh had never really experienced this sort of freedom before.

In Melbourne, his movements were closely monitored and sometimes even directed by his Mum – it didn't really matter if he was upstairs playing on his iPad, or at a friend's house. His Mum needed to know what he was doing, AT ALL TIMES. She rationalised this by saying that "the world was a dangerous place."

Was the world less scary here? Josh wondered. Everyone did seem to know each other in the Village, and they also appeared to trust one other... They seemed to trust children too.

The roads were unsealed, and bore no signposts to indicate the distance to the next town. This made it hard for Josh to know where they were. The group, however, kept marching on, as if they had made this trip many times before…

The surrounding hills and narrow valleys had been well nourished with rainfall. There were sudden changes in elevation which made it feel like steep climbing, in parts. Josh began to tire a few hours into the journey.

He knew he was not really that "fit". This had been scientifically demonstrated quite recently, in fact, when his Step-Dad had given Josh his Fit-Bit to wear for a day. Brett had been trying to prove his fitness to his boss at work, so that his insurance premium could be lowered. Brett could only do this by documenting how many steps he could do, so he had handed his device to his son. *It was cheating, really*, thought Josh, but he didn't want to be the one to point that out to his Step-Dad. As it turned out, Brett had been woefully disappointed with Josh's number of steps; and declared that Josh was an "indoors" kind of kid… and of no use to him.

In this hilly terrain, the donkeys had no trouble keeping up the pace, treading steadfastly, and regularly calling out to one another with long bellowing calls. It was a joyful group that kept to the rocky path, long since overgrown with reeds, prickly shrubs and bramble bushes.

Just as they neared a natural spring, the group stopped for lunch. The boys were treated to a delicious banquet of soft, flat bread, topped with hummus dip, olives, pickled vegetables and white, salty cheese. A yummy dessert then followed. Josh carefully picked up a golden sticky "parcel" made of delicate golden pastry. It was filled with pistachios and walnuts, and sweetened by honey.

"Awesome!" Josh exclaimed, licking his fingers appreciatively. The women smiled at him.

Having quenched their thirst by scooping the spring water into their cupped hands (and also washing their sticky fingers clean at the same time), the boys waited for the men to re-fill their sheepskin "bottles," before setting off again. It was getting late in the day, and the temperature was cooling down considerably.

As the group continued on their course, the path began to wind around a dangerous-looking precipice. Next to the cliff lay a deep ravine filled with little more than dirt and rock. Josh noticed that the adults slowed down and looked about them in a cautious manner. Perhaps they were checking to see if there were any murderers lurking about… Maybe, things were just as scary in this part of the world after all, Josh thought.

It turned out, though, that the adults were simply scouting around for a place to pitch their tents and settle down to sleep for the night.

"I hope we move away from here," Josh told Jacob.

It was so high up, he was worried he might thrash about during his sleep and accidentally tumble down to the valley below… *That would hurt, big time,* he reckoned.

Having found a suitable clearing, everyone helped to erect the tents to camp for the night. When that was done, each member of the group looked heavenward, and talked to the God in the sky. Josh looked up too. He, however, was transfixed by the magnificence of the full moon.

The next morning, at around daybreak, the group breakfasted on delicious flatbread (again) and rose petal jam before resuming their trek southwards. Pretty views of the mountains greeted them as the darkness slowly became morning, and the new day dawned. The group followed narrow paths leading through some steep cliffs, until gradually, their route was mostly made up of blind curves and sharp turns.

Josh happily trudged behind the men, when suddenly, the donkeys stopped walking and started braying loudly. Something was agitating them… The donkeys began to idle backwards until their hind legs were actually pressing against the mountainside. The men started rebuking their animals and even beating them with a stick, but to no avail. The stubborn creatures decided to lay down under their loads, and they refused to move.

The men were extremely annoyed until everyone heard what sounded like a "roar". Straining their ears to identify what was making this eerie sound, they looked about them, and that's when they saw her.

A lioness was prowling around on a nearby rock-face, growling and snarling at her human prey. She had a thick, yellowish coat, but no mane. Her most distinctive features, however, were her strong-looking jaw and her sharp teeth, which she took great satisfaction in showing off. Swift and agile, she paced about on the precipice of the adjoining mountain, swinging her tail menacingly from side to side…

While the adults and children stood only a short distance away from her, they occupied a different side of the mountain, and were physically separated by a one hundred foot drop. Despite this, the lioness could smell their fear, and she roared even more ferociously.

"Oh my God," Josh whispered, as he shuddered in fear.

CHAPTER 26: THE BAD SAMARITAN

The lioness then ventured even closer to the edge of the precipice, snarling and clawing away, as she anticipated the "kill". She was clearly frustrated by the sizeable gap that existed between the two rock ledges, but was not prepared to give up just yet.

The people were horrified, as they (too) surveyed the small distance between them and this wild beast. The young children were crying and clutching at their mother's skirts. Josh could tell, just by looking at the lioness that she knew how to hunt and eat human beings...

The lioness then made several attempts to cross to the other side. She crawled through burrows, and climbed sprawling tree branches that were hanging nearby, but it soon became apparent that she was *not* going to be able to capture her prey. She finally "puffed" in recognition of defeat, and let out a series of short roars, before angrily stomping away.

When everyone realised that they were "safe", they started to breathe normally again. The younger children continued crying, but this time, their mothers were able to pick them up and console them. Josh and Jacob looked at one other, but said nothing. (Josh had never been so frightened in all his life.)

The adults ushered the children onwards, with a heightened sense of urgency now to reach their final destination. The festive spirit they had experienced earlier was definitely over.

The group moved quickly and efficiently over the terrain, with minimal conversation. No-one joked around or laughed anymore. The mood was very sombre, as the adults kept an "ear" out for any danger which might be lurking around the next blind corner.

They heard it before they saw it. A flock of circling vultures was squawking uncontrollably at the next bend in the path. Soon, the group happened upon the body of a man lying on the ground. He was practically dead and some screeching birds were feeding off his naked corpse.

Having quickly appraised the situation, the adults moved across to the other side of the road, filing swiftly past the gruesome spectacle.

"Are we going to just leave him here?" queried Josh, alarmed.

Everyone was acting like it was *not* unusual to see a dying man on the side of the road.

"Shouldn't we try to help him… or at least, keep the birds away?" he asked despairingly.

Jacob just grabbed Josh's elbow and pulled him away, not even allowing him time to examine the man's body. Not that Josh wanted to look too closely… What he glimpsed out of the corner of his eye was ghastly enough. The worse thing, though, was that everyone wanted to get away… almost like they didn't care what happened to this man.

As they continued their ascent, the group came across other travellers heading along the same stretch of road. Josh followed quickly after them. He started to think that things might have been very different for the dying man, if only Rabboni had been here. *Rabboni would never have just left him.* Josh was sure of that.

CHAPTER 27: HA HA!

Brendan was playing outside when he suddenly remembered Josh. He missed him. As Brendan began exploring the nearby forest, he saw a tree so tall it almost reached the clouds. The tree had grown taller than the other trees he noticed, marvelling at its height. Its beautiful shady branches were really thick and long. Walking towards it, Brendan could see every kind of bird nesting in the branches above. He began to think about baby birds and how they needed their mums and dads to look after them.

Brendan was still looking up at the tree when he lost his footing, and stumbled over a huge rock. He tried to stop himself from falling by holding out his hands, but he only managed to land heavily on his outstretched wrists. He howled in pain as he lay face downwards in the dirt… until he realised that there was no one around to help him. Brendan remembered that Imma and Ally were both inside, and the other kids were playing further away. Hurt and upset, he gingerly made his way back to the house, and went looking for Imma…Brendan knew that Imma wasn't his *real* Mum, but she was pretty close.

"Imma, Imma!" Brendan cried out.

Ally heard Brendan's calls for help and came out to see what all the fuss was about.

"What happened to you?" Ally asked him sympathetically.

Ally made Brendan sit down, while she began cleaning his scratches. Imma soon materialised and began to pray for Brendan (she was clearly worried about him). She then went off in search of a green plant to gently whip against Brendan's skin. However, when Imma touched Brendan with its bristles, it stung, and Brendan started crying again. This time, he turned to Ally for comfort.

"It's ok," Ally consoled him, stroking his head gently.

A short time later, Brendan's friends came looking for him. Not surprisingly, he was ready to face the world again, and raced off instantly.

"Wait a minute!" Ally called after him. "Your shorts are all torn. You'll have to put on something else."

Brendan ran back, quickly dropped his shorts and put on the garment Imma handed to him....presumably an old pair of Jacob's.

Ally decided to stitch the hem of Brendan's linen shorts, which had come loose as a result of his fall. The needle Imma gave her was very sharp, even though it was (in actual fact) just a bit of wood splinter. *It seems to work the same way*, Ally concluded, as she slowly passed the thread through the hole, and then pushed the sharp, pointy end of the "needle" back and forth through the tough fabric.

Imma was pretty self-sufficient when it came to supplying clothing for her family. Ally had noticed Imma working away on a "loom" with weights, presumably for making new clothes. *Their fashion choices are seriously weird though*, Ally thought as she worked away, quietly.

Just as she was getting the "knack" of sewing with the wooden needle, Ally heard Imma calling her.

"Yes, Imma, I'll go and fetch water in just a bit…I'm just finishing this!" Ally then proudly showed off the "almost finished" repair-job to Imma, who examined her work before grinning at Ally and commending her for her efforts.

In truth, Ally had been putting off going to the well to collect water, after what had happened yesterday. Ally hadn't done anything differently, but she noticed that the other girls were acting strangely and whispering, presumably about her…

The communal well was the nearest collection point for all the neighbouring families. The only other source of town water was a distant reservoir…and too far away for carting water, Ally thought frowning.

When she really couldn't put it off any longer, Ally walked to the local well, clutching her jar tightly:

"Crap!" she cursed. They were all there again, the girls from yesterday… plus the "ringleader".

It suddenly dawned on Ally that she had seen this girl before. With a sudden jolt, she realised that the "Ringleader" was the girl that Aaron and his parents had visited that night.

Ally proceeded to *work* the wheel as normal, so as to avoid the scum and debris which inevitably gathered at the surface. Even though the communal well was carved out of solid rock, and sealed with clay, the water sometimes had "bits" in it.

Ally had been collecting water the way Imma had taught her, when she had first arrived in the Village. Today, however, the Ringleader wanted to draw attention to *how* Ally was drawing water, using stupid hand gestures to mimic Ally's technique. The other girls immediately began to laugh at Ally. Ally tried to ignore them as she continued working, despite being able to hear them all giggling.

The Ringleader then walked right up to Ally, and asked her to *demonstrate* for them. Ally was mortified. She dropped her vessel on the rocky soil, spilling its contents, and hurriedly ran past the snickering girls. Ally didn't stop until she found herself at the lake, on the promenade between the water and the closest dwellings. She sunk down into the sand, burying her head in her arms.

Nearby, there were some men washing and repairing their fishing equipment. One of them stopped dead in his tracks when he spotted Ally. Suddenly Aaron was right next to her. Sensing that something was terribly wrong, he crouched down to find out what was troubling Ally. Aaron's expression was so filled with tenderness and compassion that the mere sight of him, made Ally burst into tears. Aaron quickly gathered her up in his tanned, muscular arms and held her close.

Ally couldn't explain what had happened at the well, but she didn't really need to. Aaron didn't say anything. He just held her against his chest, as she cried. In time, he pulled her face back a little, to wipe away her salty tears.

Ally's vision was clouded by the weeping but she could still feel the soft caress of his fingertips against her swollen cheeks. Aaron's hands smelled of fish, salt and sweat. His smell comforted her.

Some men, however, looked disturbed at the sight of Aaron and Ally together. Av's hired hands immediately stopped sorting the tilapia fish from the scaleless catfish and stared at the young couple. One of them ran to find Av.

CHAPTER 28: NO WAY!

When Av made his way to the small customs office adjacent to the port in order to pay for his catch, he was greeted by a large queue of angry fishermen and other men involved in interregional trade. It seemed that the Tax Officer who normally processed their catch had left the Customs booth. Apparently, he had last been seen with Rabboni, and no-one knew if he was ever coming back.

The Government had tried to find a replacement for him but it turned out that few people wanted his job. The money was good… *really good*….and it wasn't a tough "gig". All you had to do was open people's boxes or bundles, check the contents, ascribe a value and write out a ticket. Easy. The *fun* bit started when you had to collect the tax money from the burly fishermen. It seemed that this group was never happy about parting with their hard-earned coins.

The "Temp" manning the booth today was still *in training*, and as such, was taking an enormous amount of time to process everyone's fish. Consequently, the fishermen were really annoyed at the long wait. They all had better things to do with their time.

The truth be told, there was no love lost between the fishermen and the tax collectors... Probably because everyone knew that tax collectors were crooks, charging honest people exorbitant sums of money on behalf of the Government...money which coincidentally always managed to find its way into their individual pockets. The fishermen couldn't prove it, but they *knew*.

In fact, the Tax Officer who had recently absconded had all the latest "mod cons" - a large home with mosaic-tiled floors, a fast horse, fine linen clothing embroidered with his initials, a silk coat (he usually kept this for private, indoor use). He even had his eye on some leather sandals spotted while travelling abroad, reproductions of ones found in the tomb of Tutankhamun with soles made of fine reeding. He was also the only guy in town with state-of-the-art, papyrus writing materials. (This purchase was considered a legitimate "tax deduction" for a tax collector, as it was integral to performing tax work.)

The "perks" of the job were unbelievable. However, it was a double-edged sword: the tax collectors' financial situation made all the townspeople seethe with jealousy. NO-ONE liked them. It appeared that not even God wanted to see tax collectors, and consequently, they were forbidden from entering the Temple.

The irony though, was just when the (former) Fisheries Tax Officer had seen the error of his ways and had thought about compensating the people he had ripped off, he had decided to quit his job. A sad development for the local fishermen.

As Av waited in the queue for the latest "ring in" the Government had installed in the booth, someone tapped him on his shoulder. He looked around and was surprised to see his hired hand, looking very concerned. After a hushed conversation between the two men, they agreed that the hired hand would take Av's place in the queue, while Av backtracked towards the foreshore. It appeared that Av had more pressing matters to attend to…

As he walked, Av looked up and said:

"Avi slach lahem ki eynam yod'im ma hem 'osim." *(Father, forgive them, for they know not what they do.)*

Av quickly spotted the culprits, nestled together on the beach. He walked straight over to Ally and spoke sternly:

"Talitha kumi". *(Little girl, I say to you, get up.)*

Ally looked up, surprised by the harsh tone in Av's voice. She had no idea what was going on.

Av continued in an authoritative tone… this time, addressing Aaron:

"Tetelestai." *(It is finished).*

Aaron was shocked to hear his Dad rebuking him. (Av clearly did not want his hired hands to understand what he was saying, and had now switched to Greek.)

Recovering slightly from this ambush, Aaron studied his father's face. There was a dark scowl spreading over the man's usual pleasant demeanour.

Aaron appealed to his Dad to understand that he and Ally were not doing anything *wrong.*

"Abba!" (Dad!) he argued, getting to his feet…but it seemed to make no difference.

Aaron recognised the steely resolve in his Father's eyes, and was crushed. He felt like something had literally died inside of him. (Aaron was not accustomed to disappointing his father. Av was normally so proud of him.)

Av then grabbed his son by the arm, to steer him away from Ally.

"Noli me tangere!" Aaron retorted. (*Do not interfere!*)

Av, however, was not deterred by his son's show of defiance. He leaned in towards him and angrily tapped his finger against his head, cursing Aaron:

"Raca!" *(You empty-headed idiot!)*

At that precise moment, Aaron knew that his father would never change his mind. Feeling completely humiliated, Aaron lowered his head and muttered:

"Anee tzameh." *(I'm thirsty.)* "Eshkerah" *(I need a strong drink.)*

Aaron then stormed off, leaving Ally alone with Av. Distressed, Ally anxiously looked from Aaron back to Av.

"Av, I don't understand why you're so upset with us….or with me…I thought you and Imma… liked me?" she stammered.

Ally's appeal fell on deaf ears. Av did not acknowledge her at all, but turned his face away from her.

Feeling totally shunned, Ally got up and hurried away, in the opposite direction to Aaron. Out of the corner of his eye, Av watched her leave before looking up again and pleading:

"Hosanna!" *(O LORD, save us!)*

Meanwhile, Aaron found himself in the hinterland. He really wasn't sure how he had gotten there. He was angered by his father's treatment of him. *Why can't my father understand about Ally?* Aaron asked himself. *And why is he so set against her, anyway? Doesn't he know that I love her?*

A million thoughts raced around Aaron's head as he considered his predicament. He paced around for a while, feeling like a lost sheep. Aaron really couldn't think clearly. His brain was all muddled up...

Glancing around to check that no-one was within earshot, Aaron desperately called out at the top of his lungs:

"Eli, Eli, lama sabachthani!?" *(My God, my God, why have you forsaken me?)*

CHAPTER 29: HAPPY FEET

Having travelled for three days, the tired-looking party finally reached a small hilltop. Perched high on the mountain before them stood Yerushalayim like a glorious throne. Everyone in the group stopped to gaze at the impressive city. After a few seconds of admiring the view, the group resumed their walk with renewed joy… the large walled city in shimmering white beckoned them onwards.

Josh was really tired, even though he and the other kids had taken turns riding on the donkey – it turned out that only kids or women were allowed to ride donkeys (he had discovered with delight). He had never ridden a donkey before.

This brown donkey plodded along at a constant, steady pace. He would not be hurried, even when Josh gave him a light slap on his bottom. After an hour or so, Josh dismounted, and let some of the other kids have a go. The ride was ok, but it was not *that* exciting… the donkey travelled *so* slowly.

The adult men had no option but to walk. Josh admired these guys, who resolutely kept moving along the dusty tracks, setting a consistent pace for everyone else. The men never complained, Josh noticed.

As the group continued onwards, they were suddenly joined by other pilgrims who appeared to be heading in the same direction. Some of these people were even singing cheerful songs and playing harps and cymbals. To add to the mini "orchestra", the nearby city also resounded with a loud blast of a trumpet. Josh recalled hearing a similar-sounding horn back in Jacob's Village, the night of the dinner party…

"Hey look at all these people!" exclaimed Josh.

Jacob just grinned back at him, knowingly. All sorts of people were now converging on their path, making jubilant strides towards the city wall and its impressive gates.

"WOW! There are thousands of people here," Josh uttered, gobsmacked.

The last time Josh had seen so many people was at the Royal Melbourne Show. He remembered how he had to nervously "shadow" his parents, in case he lost sight of them. Fortunately, his family had managed to stay together on that day (despite the many "distractions"), but there had been a constant feeling of apprehension in the pit of Josh's stomach as he had navigated through the noisy throng of people. Josh didn't like crowds.

It was a different story today. Even though Josh knew no one (apart from Jacob and the family friends) he wasn't overwhelmed by all the noise. There was no pushing or shoving (like at the Melbourne Show). Everyone was smiling and chatting excitedly to one another. People were full of excitement and anticipation…

The children and the grown-ups alike joined in the party atmosphere, singing at the top of their voices. Josh noticed men and women helping the old people, who were generally slower-moving as they happily shuffled along with their canes.

The noise we're making can probably be heard for miles, he thought gleefully. Surveying the crowds as they trod along in unison, it was almost as if they were ALL one big, happy family.

At the fountain gate, after they had finished washing in the natural spring, they continued up the steps that would lead them to their final destination. However, just as they hit the city wall, on the eastern side, the group was suddenly confronted by an unexpected scene…

The first sign that something was wrong was the sight of women huddled together, crying bitterly. Some people were even throwing dust on their heads. Others were rolling in the dirt, and sobbing loudly.

The women's shouts and cries almost managed to drown out another sound, altogether more sinister…a flock of black crows screeched and cawed overhead. Josh looked across and saw some tall wooden beams erected close to where the women stood, just near the city gates. Three men were hanging off these poles, each man pinned to a separate wooden cross.

The men were only barely alive, their lungs straining to extract precious air. Each inhalation, however, seemed to make them groan in fresh agony.

As Josh got closer, he could see that their bodies were completely covered with open wounds, their faces darkened and bruised as blood seeped down their weakened frames, eventually falling to the ground and creating a murky puddle. Masses of red blood also stained their private parts. That's when Josh realised that the men were completely naked.

"Oh my God!" exclaimed Josh, gaping in horror.

All three victims were scrambling to stretch out just so they could breathe, but they couldn't really move much, because of the long, protruding nails which fastened their feet in place. There was a sign posted above the men's heads, with fine, spidery writing on it. Josh strained to read it but he couldn't.

The blood at the scene mirrored the bright red uniforms worn by the soldiers who guarded the three men. The soldiers thrusted their silvery shields at the crowds intermittently, to prevent the shrieking women from getting too close.

Each soldier gripped a sharpened spear in his right hand, while routinely shouting terse orders to the noisy crowd. Onlookers were under no illusion that serious reprisals would result, if the soldiers were not obeyed. Josh's pulse quickened.

The soldiers glared menacingly at the spectators. Only the soldiers' eyes and mouths could be seen beneath their helmets. Their grey metal head gear had curved side panels which covered most of their face. Josh studied them nervously. Protective metal armour around their shoulders, arms and legs was fastened with hooks and laces. A belt secured around their waist acted as a holder for their polished sword and their "skirt", made up of overlapping leather strips, heavily studded with metal. When the soldiers kicked at some stray dogs which were trying to lick the pool of blood on the ground, Josh noticed that even the soldiers' sandals were strengthened with iron hobnails.

Josh averted his eyes. He could not stand to look at this chilling scene any longer. And such, ended the happy march, near the entrance gate of the city.

CHAPTER 30: THE PALACE

The children were quickly ushered away by their chaperones. The adults were clearly impacted by the shocking scene. The women hid their faces behind their scarves as they walked away with unusual haste.

Josh followed the women, but he couldn't resist sneaking a final look at the men hanging... Their faces were so twisted and disfigured, they were almost past recognition. They seriously didn't look human anymore.

WHY are they being killed? What had they done? His stomach churned uncomfortably.

The family continued to head to the left, along the top of the wall. Upon entering the city proper, the group was immediately engulfed into a large swarm of people, coming and going in every direction. Everyone went about their business, almost like they didn't know that on the other side of the wall, three men were being impaled alive.

The city was a thriving metropolis and incredibly noisy. High-ranking cavalry officers were everywhere. Josh also noticed important-looking men with sashes tied around their waists and fancy turbans on their heads, and women with heavy eyeshadow, and even heavier perfume. There were lots of beggars kneeling before the visitors, with their calloused, wrinkly hands outstretched and their heads humbly bowed, waiting for any charitable contributions to come their way.

Merchandise was being carted around on people's backs. At one point, Josh was almost run over by a large wheeled cage as it came hurtling towards him. He moved back just in time, locking eyes briefly with a young passenger (about his age) who was trapped inside the cage. The boy was clinging on for dear life. *Are people getting sold too?* Josh wondered anxiously.

Josh got a strong whiff of wheat, honey, olive oil and various exotic spices. Merchants were spruiking loudly for potential customers, offering "deals" on luxurious clothing, purple cloth and embroidery, brightly coloured carpets, well-made cords and ropes, jewels and even gold. Caged lambs, sheep and goats were bleating and whining away, as they underwent a thorough inspection by the shrewd shoppers.

The ever-present soldiers in red uniforms stood nearby guarding the city's towers, and keeping a close watch on the townspeople. Their shields hung menacingly on the walls behind them.

"Are we booked into a hotel tonight, or are we still camping outside?" Josh quizzed Jacob.

For the first time in a while, Josh was not keen on camping outdoors, even with the chance to observe another luminous full moon. Ironically, the presence of soldiers made Josh feel decidedly *unsafe*.

Jacob pointed towards a temple, straight ahead of them. Josh looked up to see a wonderfully opulent building. It had white palatial steps leading up to an impressive gateway entrance, and it was surrounded by enormous square doorposts.

"Wow! That's sick... Are we staying there?" Josh asked expectantly. "It looks like it was built for a King or something! Can we afford that?"

Jacob, however, didn't answer him. He looked uncharacteristically gloomy.

As the family neared the external wall of the temple, Josh could see carvings of palm trees and winged creatures on the wall facing the street. The decorative palm trees alternated with the angelic creatures, one following the other, all the way around the wall.

Unfortunately, though, the adults selected the place *next door* as their intended place of accommodation… a building that was pretty "down-market", more like a hostel than a hotel. Judging by the people entering, it seemed to attract other weary, sweaty travellers who were desperately looking for shelter (just like them).

Jacob's friends made the necessary arrangements with the "Hotel" staff, and they were soon ushered into small, sparsely furnished rooms.

"Well, it's not the Palace… but at least we're indoors," Josh quipped, looking tentatively around the dimly-lit room.

Jacob started to put his things away, and Josh helped him. He knew Jacob was still upset by what they had witnessed earlier. He too felt a deep sadness for the men, and was more than a little afraid.

"Jacob, this is Yeru-shala-yim, isn't it…you know, the place where Rabboni is staying? Let's try and find him quickly. The sooner we locate him, the sooner we can get back home. K?"

Jacob shrugged his shoulders and continued unpacking, while some of the adults left the hotel, in search of breakfast. The city appeared to have a ready supply of freshly-baked flatbread, which sat cooking on outdoor "griddles".

The adults soon returned with deliciously-warm bread, which they promptly offered to the boys. (The bread was particularly tasty when dipped in the tangy vinegar.) This was followed by some dark raisin cake, and a plentiful supply of sun-dried dates and walnuts, just to finish off. After guzzling down some grape juice syrup, Josh and Jacob were officially ready to start their search, and they nervously ventured outside…

"Hey, lots of people are heading inside the palace. Why don't we start there?" suggested Josh.

The boys slowly made their way through the gate into what they discovered was the outer courtyard of the massive temple. When they finally reached the official entrance, they spotted some men washing the carcasses of animals.

"Oh Ma-aate! You can't be serious?" Josh said gobsmacked. Were they really using this amazing building as a slaughterhouse? Josh was really confused.

Within this entrance room were four sturdy tables made of cut stone, two on each side of the room. What happened next, however, began to terrify Josh.

"Are you kidding me?" Josh exclaimed loudly.

He knew that meat actually *came* from real animals being butchered… but he had never watched it being performed. Now, right in front of his eyes, men were grabbing frenzied pigeons out of a wooden cage, one by one, and before each pigeon had sufficient time to fully extend its wings, its neck was wringed with clinical precision. The carcasses were then placed on another table, allowing the blood to be drained out from the birds. Another worker was grabbing the wings, while tearing open the bird's body (but still leaving the wings intact).

The odour coming from the tables was absolutely disgusting, despite the fact that the equipment used to kill was kept on one table, in a very ordered way, while the bloodied carcasses were piled up high on a separate table.

Strangely enough, Jacob did not look concerned by this macabre activity, almost like he had seen it many times before. When Josh turned to him, Jacob simply pointed to the carcasses and said: "Khat-aw-aw."

"What do you mean? I don't get it."

"Avon," Jacob added, as if this would explain everything.

Josh still had no idea what his friend was trying to tell him. (He wasn't absolutely sure he wanted to know.)

"Why don't we get out of here…it's really creepy," Josh whispered, looking around him…

"Barak." Jacob tried again, this time he kneeled down, as if trying to demonstrate someone worshipping.

"I don't get what killing an animal has to do with a U.S. Ex-President. Let's just go….*please*?" Josh implored his friend.

Jacob was now lying prostrate on the ground, his head lifting occasionally to see whether Josh understood his version of "charades". Josh, however, was too distracted by the men covered in blood.

Eventually, Jacob gave up on the "play-acting" and got to his feet. As the boys began walking out of the slaughter house, Josh stopped to salute the door-man at the end of the passageway:

"See-yas!" he said sarcastically.

Just as the boys were about to exit the building, they heard a lot of noise and a flurry of activity, coming from somewhere behind them. They turned around to see lots of people running inside. Intrigued by all the commotion, the boys decided to follow the people and investigate…

Through the intricate maze of rooms, they discovered a group of men huddled around some heavy-looking material, scratching their heads. The material had apparently fallen from the high ceiling and was now lying before them, evenly split in two pieces. With no curtains in place to partition the area, the boys (and everyone else) could easily see into the inner recesses of the temple, altogether fancier and more ornate in style. Jacob couldn't believe his eyes.

"C'MON, Jacob. It's nothing. Let's just go!"

Josh was definitely glad to be leaving the "palace."

CHAPTER 31: ON SHAKY GROUND

Just as the boys were finally clear of the building, the ground started shaking from beneath them.   There was a strange sound just before the stone pavement began to uproot and crack up, and every person was immediately jolted from where they stood.

Josh and Jacob were still in the temple courtyard, itself surrounded by extensive porticos and gigantic columns. They both clung to each other in order to steady themselves, when they again heard that unmistakeable large, creaking sound coming from the surrounding walls.

"RUN, JACOB! QUICK!" Josh yelled.

Josh had never experienced an earthquake before, but his natural instinct just "kicked in" and he grabbed Jacob's arm and made a dash for the street. In Australia, earthquakes rarely caused any damage, or at least anything that would feature on *YouTube*. He remembered, however, learning about a massive earthquake in Japan, which struck at Fukushima unleashing a savage tsunami, and causing extensive damage to the nuclear power plant (not to mention heaps of people dying). His mind drifted temporarily to Jacob's coastal village and Ally and Brendan, as he thought about tsunami waves…

He was quickly brought back to reality by all the screaming. People everywhere were running out of buildings, and huddling close together on the city streets.

Chariots too were dashing wildly past the crowds through the pathways, and rushing back and forth in the city squares. Some people had fallen down in their haste to leave, and were crying out for help.

Josh and Jacob tried to sprint, but their bodies kept swaying, slowing them down considerably… Soldiers were being summoned, but even they appeared to stumble as they pressed forward towards the crowds.

When the boys were finally clear of the temple, they looked at one other, dumbstruck. They had no idea what to do next… Their hearts melted with fear, their knees trembled: it felt like all their strength was gone.

Around them, people's faces were pale with fright. The whole city was in a state of sheer pandemonium. It felt like it was the end of the world.

And just when the earth stopped shaking, the sun turned black as ink. The sky just disappeared, almost like a book being snapped shut as darkness quickly descended around them. Within seconds, it was impossible to see anything. Josh looked around and suddenly realised that Jacob was no longer there.

"JACOB, where are you?" he called out frantically.

His call, however, went unanswered, as the noise level of the street was now deafening, and seemed to eclipse his own raised voice. Josh started to move about, searching for his friend, mindful of tripping over the rubble that the earthquake had caused. Lots of buildings had been smashed; the roads themselves had cracked open, and were dangerously uneven.

Everyone was "spooked"…even the horses whinnied and made their riders crazy. Women and children were howling and crying out for help.

The merchants too were distressed. Ten minutes earlier, people had been appraising their wares: gold, silver, precious stones and pearls; linen, purple cloth, silk and scarlet cloth; the rare woods and objects made of ivory, bronze, iron and marble; and cinnamon, spice, incense, myrrh, and frankincense; wine and oil, flour and wheat, cattle and sheep, horses and carriages, slaves, even human lives. All trading had now stopped.

Josh was sure that it was around lunchtime, the middle of the day. And yet, it was so dark. A solar eclipse could (technically) cause sudden darkness, but that was impossible at this time of the month when the moon was full. A full moon could simply NOT get in the way between the Earth and the Sun. (He knew that a Solar Eclipse could only occur during the time of a *New* Moon – not a *full* moon.)

Part of Josh was hoping that he was wrong, and that it *was* an eclipse, as he knew that a total solar eclipse would only last for 7 minutes and 31.1 seconds. Light would then return. Josh decided to wait it out.

Soon, he noticed oil lamps bobbing around, as the residents prepared themselves for the darkness. Josh fixed his gaze on the soft lights floating around him in mid-air, and decided to follow one of these lights, until it arrived at the main road. There he noticed overturned tables and benches, where previously moneychangers and merchants had sat. Animals had been released from their cages, and were now free to roam the area, but surprisingly, these creatures had chosen to loiter close to their cages. Their confused calls and squawks simply added to the general cacophony.

Josh spotted some people looting from one particular table. He moved closer to see what they were grabbing. *Good God - they're oil lamps,* Josh thought excitedly.

Josh pushed his way into the throng of people and "pinched" one of the small devices. It had a wide discus base, a narrow shoulder but no handle. Josh knew it was stealing, but under the circumstances, he thought it would be ok. (He rationalised that he could always return on a different occasion, and repay the money.)

Another looter then helped Josh light his lamp by rubbing their flax wick sticks together and then pouring some olive oil into the "bowl". It was so reassuring to possess light once more. Josh felt better instantly and set about trying to find Jacob.

CHAPTER 32: BURIED ALIVE

Moving further along the street, Josh came across many frightened people desperately searching for missing friends or family members. Wherever Josh turned, it appeared that there was deep anguish and bitter weeping... A woman nearby was trying to comfort her friend "Rachel" who was weeping for her children, but she refused to be comforted for her children were gone.

With the use of his lamp, Josh began to walk in the direction of where he thought the Palace might be. He thought that Jacob might have possibly returned to the Hotel, right next door.

With renewed conviction, Josh found his way there, only to discover that the Hotel had been flattened by the earthquake. All that remained were a pile of stones… He hoped that his friends had left in time, but he couldn't be sure.

Suddenly, someone tapped him on the shoulder. He turned around to see Jacob grinning at him. Jacob then grabbed him in a bear hug. (Josh had never been so relieved in his entire life.)

Once they had exchanged tales of where they had been during the darkness, Josh pointed to the rubble that lay before them, and said authoritatively:

"C'mon, Jacob. We need to start moving these rocks. Our friends could be under there… buried alive!"

Jacob didn't look convinced.

"Jacob, I'm sure they didn't leave the Hotel. When we headed out, I saw the women getting dinner ready. We've got to look for them… and quickly."

Sensing Josh's determination to press ahead, Jacob quickly relented.

"Kephas?" (*Rock?*) Jacob asked, scratching his head. Jacob wasn't sure if the boys could lift the heavy boulders that had now collected on the site.

"We can do it together. C'mon!" Josh reassured him.

Without wasting another minute, the boys got to work, and began lifting the debris slowly and carefully. Working side by side, they were able to lift even some of the larger boulders and cart them away.

Josh's oil lamp provided several hours of light, and the boys used the time wisely, concentrating their efforts on where they believed the bedrooms would be located. Gradually, the boys managed to pilfer through a significant amount of rubble. They never stopped to take a break, but continued their back-breaking work, one hefty rock at a time.

And just as their oil lamp flickered its last glint of light, the sun re-appeared. The boys glanced around them, sensing that something was different. They suddenly realised that the darkness had lifted. Just like that. Undeterred, Josh and Jacob continued their gruelling work.

A few wild dogs appeared by their side, sniffing about and occasionally barking, as if they were picking up a scent… Some people heard the dogs' barking and began noticing the boys' activity. Pretty soon, several men decided to join Josh and Jacob in their search.

More and more people began appearing and lending their assistance, and within a short time, there was a proper work crew in place. The boys were no longer alone.

They were also not alone when the family members were pulled out of the rubble, all covered in powdery white dust, but miraculously unhurt. The work crew cheered loudly and shouted with joy each time another person was lifted out of the debris, heightening the emotions of the swelling crowd that had gathered to watch.

The rescuers continued to slog away, summoning fresh energy with each new "recovery".

Finally, when all the family members had been accounted for, there was rapturous applause and enthusiastic pats on the back for the rescuers. These men, however, looked round to find Josh and Jacob, whose example and service they wanted to publicly recognise. The men embraced and congratulated each boy in turn.

Josh was tired and thirsty, but extremely happy. Many lives had been saved that day… He had been rewarded for his faith.

CHAPTER 33: BACK TO SCHOOL

Imma knew that something was up. Ally had arrived home looking exceptionally sad. Despite her downcast appearance, though, Ally had gotten "stuck into" her chores.

Imma watched as Ally scrubbed the family's clothes with meticulous care. This job was solitary in nature and, as such, involved no interaction with others (so Imma couldn't properly ascertain what was going on with Ally), but the fact that Ally had put the family's needs before her own emotional state, earned her a new measure of respect... It seemed to Imma that the girl who had peered into her window only a few short weeks ago, had grown up a lot.

At that moment, Brendan stomped into the room and interrupted Imma's thoughts. Imma smiled, and decided to go and check that the embers were still burning in the courtyard.

"Ally, where's Josh? Is he coming home soon?" Brendan pestered his older sister.

He had been looking for Ally to ask about Josh' whereabouts. There were other kids to play with (his own age), but Brendan really missed his older brother.

"He'll be back soon. You know he's looking for Rabboni; that might take some time…" Ally responded reassuringly.

"But that's what you said yesterday. I want to see him now!" Brendan argued.

Secretly, Ally hoped Josh's efforts had already proved fruitful. She was more than ready to leave the Village. In fact, for the first time since they had arrived, Ally was hoping against hope that Rabboni really was the answer to their problems, and could help them return home. Without his involvement, she couldn't see any other way out.

"Ally, I've got heaps to tell him. Some kids and I dug a hole in the woods and buried some secret treasure! Oh…and Imma taught me how to count in a different language. I reckon, I'll be ready for school when we get back," Brendan bragged, clearly proud of all his recent achievements.

Ally had not thought about School in a while. She had been planning to study another language (Greek) and Ancient History next year, before her life had taken an unexpected turn... She didn't really know which language was being spoken around here, but surprisingly, she had developed an understanding of it, in a relatively short space of time. At the very least, she knew what was expected of her, and she also knew when she had broken the rules.

Imma had been very patient with Ally, and kind, and Av had been easy to get along with too, up until this afternoon… Village life was certainly different to what she knew, but in some ways, it was OK. There was always someone around (usually Imma) to help you with "stuff". *Learning Greek shouldn't be too hard*, she reasoned, *if I ever need to.*

"Brendan, would you like to learn how to read...in English?" Ally asked a surprised Brendan.

"OK," he answered eagerly. "Will you teach me?"

"Sure. We could make a start now, if you like."

Brendan was overjoyed. He clapped his hands excitedly, beaming with joy.

"What are you going to teach me?" he asked impatiently, trailing after her, as Ally ventured outside.

"Well, first, we'll need to find a sharp stick, for our 'pen'. And perhaps we can use the ground as our 'paper'."

Brendan scurried around, collecting an extensive array of long sticks, from which to choose the appropriate writing instrument.

"Ok, why don't we start with the alphabet?" Ally announced.

She began to draw a large "A" in the ground, and then encouraged Brendan to copy her design. Together, they huddled over a bit of earth, just outside the vegetable garden, and English lessons commenced in earnest. In fact they were both so absorbed in the lesson, neither one of them noticed Av and Aaron returning home.

CHAPTER 34: THE POET

When Av arrived home that night, it was with a heavy heart. Aaron had eventually returned to the shore to help the crew clean-up for the day, but he had barely looked at his Father. In fact, the two men had not spoken the whole journey home.

How can I possibly get through to my son, Av wondered, *that Ally is simply not a suitable bride? Come to that, why do I (as the father and the head of the house) have to offer an explanation at all? My "word" should be respected and obeyed by all family members!*

When they neared their home, Imma came out to greet the men. At once, she knew that "things" were not right between them.

Looking at Aaron's downcast appearance, she called out: "Bni!" (*My son*)!

Imma affectionately took Aaron's arm and quickly led him inside. Once they had reclined in the living room, Imma looked deeply into her son's despairing face and waited for him to open up his heart to her.

"Mayim rabim lo yukhlu lekhabot et ha'ahavah, uneharot lo yishtephuha!" (*Many waters cannot quench love, neither can floods drown it!)* Aaron declared loud enough for his Dad to hear.

Av decided he had heard more than enough... As he exited the room in disgust, Av shook his head, thinking: *This is my son, listen to him!*

Imma waited for her husband to leave, before gently prodding:

"Ani Lo Mevinah." *(I don't understand.)* "Mah dodekh midod, hayaphah banashim?" *(What is it about your loved one that is better than any other?)*

They both knew that Ally was the topic of discussion.

"Keshoshanah ben hachochim,ken ra'ayati ben habanot," *(A lily among thorns, so is my beloved as compared with any other girls,)* Aaron responded, without hesitating.

At that moment, it became abundantly clear to Imma that her son had very strong feelings for Ally.

"Ani lo Yoda'at..." *(I don't know...)* Imma continued tenderly. "Mah techezeh bashulamit?" *(Why should you seek a mere Shulammite?)*

Aaron closed his eyes, wondering how he could properly convey the depth of emotion he felt for Ally. How could he possibly make his Mother understand that he was now a man, with grownup feelings? Aaron knew that until recently, he spoke and thought and reasoned as a child did. But now that he had become a man, his thoughts grew beyond those of his childhood, and he had since put away the childish things…

"Lo yada'ti naphshi samatni markevot ami nadiv," Aaron recited. *(Before I was aware, my desire had made me as the chariots of my noble people.)* (Aaron had studied a lot of poetry in the Temple, when he was younger.)

Imma stared at her son. He looked the same, but he sounded like a much wiser man.

Imma then said what she always said in situations that were too hard for her to solve:

"Im yirtzeh Hashem…" *(If God is willing…)*

Aaron managed a half-smile for his Mum and said:

"Ani ohev otach." (*I love you.*)

She then reached across and kissed him on the cheek, responding:

"Ani ohevet otkha!" (*I love you!*)

There was nothing more to be said. As Aaron got to his feet to wash up for dinner, Ally happened to look up from her teaching. She suddenly saw Aaron gazing at her through the latticed window, and her heart simply melted.

Later that night, Ally found herself searching through the town for the one she loves… but he wasn't there. She looked on every street, but he wasn't there. She even asked the guards patrolling the town: "Have you seen the one I love so much?" Right after that, she found him. She held him and would not let him go until she had taken him to the home of her mother…" Then Ally woke up.

Argh…It was just another crazy dream, she sighed.

After that, Ally could not return to sleep for a very long time.

Aaron, too, had difficulties sleeping that night…so, early in the morning, (before the rooster had even crowed) he decided to "visit" Ally.

He crept downstairs and watched Ally sleep for a minute before lightly tapping her on the shoulder. When Ally's squinty eyes finally rested on him, Aaron beckoned her to follow him downstairs. Ally didn't know if she was still dreaming…but she quickly rose to her feet and the two of them headed out quietly.

When they were out of the family's earshot, Aaron turned to Ally and took her hands in his. He had been practising what he would tell her all night.

Aaron cleared his throat before beginning:

"Libavtini achoti khalah, libavtini be'achat me'eynayikh; be'achad 'anak mitsavronayikh." *(You have ravished my heart, my lovely one, my bride; I am overcome by one glance of your eyes; by a single chain of your necklace.)*

Ally knew Aaron was deadly serious; the desperate longing in his eyes, giving him away.

"Aaron - I know… but I am terribly homesick. I think I need to be back among my own people," Ally confessed.

Last night's dream had only managed to make her yearning for Melbourne grow even stronger. Sensing that Ally was holding back without sufficient cause, Aaron knew that he had to "up the ante":

"Kchini imakh venarutsah!" *(Take me with you; come let's run!)*

"I don't think I can take you with me," Ally protested.

Ally then remembered a romantic verse she had been required to learn at School. She had never really understood the poet's words, until now:

"Perhaps you can seal me in your heart with permanent betrothal, for love is as strong as death…" Ally recited from memory.

Not wanting to accept defeat, Aaron lifted her trembling hand to his lips and kissed it softly. He then whispered:

"Ahava le'olam lo nichshelet." *(Love never fails.)*

CHAPTER 35: THE RICH SAD RULER

Following the earthquake, the travellers were naturally faced with the task of finding another hotel. The townspeople, however, would hear none of it. In fact, the residents fell over themselves trying to offer their own particular brand of hospitality, and one after the other, strangers urged and pleaded with the family to stay with them. (It still surprised Josh how these foreigners were prepared to open up their homes to perfect strangers…)

Both boys were soon billeted by a respectable man, dressed in purple, who arrived in a horse-drawn chariot. *He looks really important,* Josh thought.

The man introduced himself as "Jonathan" and seemed determined to host as many people as possible. At his bequest, servants ran to and from his villa, organising transportation for the many invited guests.

Before they knew it, Josh and Jacob were standing in a small chariot behind a "driver", being escorted by two horses at a very quick pace. The chariot's floor was only a loosened mesh of stretched rope – it was really fun to ride in, as the boys tried to anticipate the next bump in the road.

Fortunately, Jonathon's home had not been affected by the earthquake – an imposing residence of white limestone soon welcomed the weary travellers. The grand villa was surrounded by tall cypress trees and sections of olive groves. It was the picture of serenity.

"Cool!   This is more like it," Josh exclaimed.

He couldn't wait to get inside and explore the various rooms. Once the horsemen hitched the halter shanks on the posts beside the villa, the visitors were all ushered inside…   The boys followed the house servant through the labyrinth of rooms, staring at the white plastered walls adorned with woven silken tapestries, and the intricate mosaic-tiled floors.

Josh and Jacob could not believe their luck. And it just got better… After they had all washed their hands, the boys were led into an actual bathroom. And sitting right in the centre of the spacious room was a sunken stone bathtub, filled with warm clean water to soak in.

Josh hadn't seen a real bathtub in so long… This one was more like a Jacuzzi. He figured it could easily hold about five people. It didn't take him long to strip down to his underwear and submerge in the sunken pool.

"C'mon, it's AWESOME!" he called out to Jacob, who followed within seconds.

Jacob and Josh exchanged satisfied smiles as they splashed around and enjoyed the soothing water. A male servant hovering nearby picked up the boys' dirty clothing from the floor, whilst another servant arrived with two fresh towels and identical silk robes, which were left on the stone steps (presumably for the boys to change into).

"Can you believe this?" Josh called out excitedly, looking around the opulent bathroom.

Jacob chatted away non-stop, clearly enjoying himself too. The boys remained in the tub until their skin started to look all wrinkly, and their tummies started to make strange sounds, alerting them to another important matter... dinner.

When a servant entered the bathroom to announce that the evening meal was ready, the boys knew it was time to exit the tub. They put on their robes and made their way through the long corridor, where they were met by yet another (female) servant with a pleasant face. She ushered them into the dining room, a brightly-lit open space where Jonathan sat presiding over a lavish square banquet table.

Jonathon was now dressed in a long white robe and beckoned his guests to join him on the couches which encircled the table. There were three couches in total, the fourth side of the table being left open for the servants to come and go as they needed. The adults were assigned the seats closest to their Host, while the boys were asked to sit further down the table, nearer the door.

"Isn't it great that we can just lounge around and eat? No-one even cares if you don't sit up straight," Josh told Jacob excitedly.

Jacob was busy searching for a soft cushion to rest against, and was only half-listening to Josh. At soon as everyone was comfortably seated, Jonathon shut the dining room doors, and took his place at the centre of the table. He then prayed over the food, before assigning portions to each guest.

The boys eagerly waited to receive their portion of tasty roast lamb, which they grabbed with one hand and gobbled down quickly... in between sips of spiced wine. They even had one dipping plate between them, which they thoroughly enjoyed, using their bread "spoon".

The boys' enormous appetite was soon rewarded with extra portions.

After dinner, all the guests reclined contentedly, while a group of musicians entertained them by playing various stringed instruments. The tasty food and lively music put everyone in a good mood... all except for Jonathan. He spoke quietly to the people seated nearest him, but Josh noticed that he never really smiled or joked around.

When the women got up to dance, Josh covered his mouth and said to Jacob:

"I think they're drunk."

Jacob just smiled and clapped his hands, joyfully. The other male guests appeared happy to sit back and watch the women dance, clapping their hands enthusiastically, in time with the beat. It appeared that everyone was trying their hardest to forget about what had happened earlier that day. All except for Jonathan. And as the night wore on, he looked sadder still.

CHAPTER 36: FINDING RABBONI

When the women finally resumed their seats, the men began telling jokes. It appeared that the adults had a whole stack of them. Each man stood up (in turn) and posed a riddle for all the other guests to solve… When someone did finally guess correctly, everyone would erupt into fits of laughter.

Josh knew some funny jokes (but unfortunately, they were all in English). As such, he decided to keep quiet.

When it was Jonathon's turn, he stood up before his guests and presented the following riddle:

"Vehu mecholal mipesha'enu, meduka me'avonoteynu. Musar shlomeynu 'alav, uvachavurato nirpa lanu."

(But because of our sins he was wounded, beaten because of the evil we did. We are healed by the punishment he suffered, made whole by the blows he received.)

Everyone looked at one another, in bewilderment.

Jonathon continued to tease his guests:

"Kulanu katson ta'inu, ish ledarko paninu. VAdonai hiphgi'a bo,et 'avon kulanu."

(All of us were like sheep that were lost, each of us going his own way. But the LORD made the punishment fall on him, the punishment all of us deserved.)

"Huh?" queried Jacob, scratching his head...

Josh looked around the table, realising that everyone's mood had suddenly changed. Jonathan, however, continued with his riddle:

"Nigas vehu na'aneh,velo yiphatch piv. Kase latevach yuval, ukherachel liphney gozazeha ne'elamah,velo yiphtach piv."

(He was treated harshly, but endured it humbly; he never said a word. Like a lamb about to be slaughtered, like a sheep about to be sheared, he never said a word.)

"Me'otser umimishpat lukach,ve'et doro mi yesocheach? Ki nigzar me'erets chayim, mipesha' ami nega' lamo."

(He was arrested and sentenced and led off to die, and no one cared about his fate. He was put to death for the sins of our people.)

When Jonathon had finally finished, he sat down. Everyone else then started shifting uncomfortably in their seats and lowering their gaze. No-one laughed. In fact, no-one spoke for several minutes. Eventually, though, a guest at the table responded quietly with one word:

"Eesoos."

Everyone looked down at their empty plates and fidgeted with their hands.

Josh didn't understand what was going on. He looked across at Jacob and thought that he could see Jacob tearing up... Aware that Josh's eyes were fixed on him, Jacob used the back of his hand to wipe away the tears that had unwittingly collected on his face. He didn't look at Josh.

"What's happening bro?" Josh asked. "Did something happen to Rabboni in the earthquake? Is he...*dead*?"

Everything that followed was a blur. The elation that the guests had felt earlier, of finding a lovely home to "vacation" in, had all but disappeared.

The next couple of days were strangely uneventful. Jacob just trounced around the sleeping quarters, barely speaking to anyone. Josh had never seen him looking so depressed.

Josh started to believe that something horrible must have happened to Rabboni. Nothing else could explain Jacob's tears...plus the distressed looks on people's faces at dinner that night. Jonathon's sad demeanour had infected the whole household.

Josh started to think that if Rabboni was no longer around, this whole side-trip had been a huge waste of time. It also meant that Josh was out of options. He, Ally and Brendan would be stuck in the Village… never again to return to their real home. Josh sighed despairingly, and decided to go for a walk.

It was evening now and as he proceeded through the corridor leading out to the garden, he noticed Jacob's friends busily packing up their things. *I wonder if we're heading back to the Village tomorrow*, Josh thought gloomily.

It had been several days since they had arrived in this city. Jonathon had continued to be kind to his guests, looking after their every need, but he did it with a heavy heart. He was definitely the saddest-looking person *ever*, Josh thought.

Lamps were placed on the porch outside, giving light to the lush garden. The sky overhead looked awesome (as it always did, Josh believed).

Gazing up at the moon and the stars, and imagining the galaxies far beyond this one, Josh started to feel a little better. He traced Cepheus with his finger, and thought about the star's nickname, "The King". It didn't really look like a "king"…it actually looked more like a house, Josh reckoned.

Josh's thoughts then naturally returned to his home in Melbourne. He began to wonder what his parents were doing. Were they frantically searching for their children? Had the police been contacted? Would his Mum blame *him* for going missing? Would he get yelled at? Anyway he looked at it, the future was not too bright, but there was nothing Josh could do about it.

"Don't be afraid," someone spoke from over his left shoulder.

Josh jumped with fright. He looked around to see who it was, and his jaw dropped. It was Rabboni.

CHAPTER 37: TOO GOOD TO BE TRUE

"Rabboni…is that you?" Josh stammered.

He couldn't believe his eyes. And yet, there he was, standing in the garden, barely a few feet away.

"It *is* me. Why are you so frightened?" Rabboni asked him gently.

"I heard that something had happened to you…I thought… you may have died," Josh admitted nervously.

"You can see that it is I, myself… Touch me and see; a ghost does not have flesh and bones, as you can see I have."

Josh didn't want to touch him. *This is seriously weird,* he told himself.

"It's not that weird," Rabboni responded, reading Josh's thoughts. "Josh, it was written long ago that the Messiah must suffer and die and rise again from the dead on the third day… and that this message of salvation should be taken from Jerusalem to all the nations: There is forgiveness of sins for all who turn to me."

Josh just stood there, with his mouth hanging open.

"Huh? You're telling me that you…DID die? And then you came back to life again?" Josh asked incredulously.

Rabboni didn't answer. He just lifted his hands and presented them before Josh. And there they were: visible marks left from the iron nails which had pinned him so cruelly to that wooden cross. Josh lowered his head. That's when he noticed fresh wounds on Rabboni's feet; bloodied, gaping holes, where once was muscle and bone…

"Oh my God! That was you?" Josh asked in disbelief. "I don't get it… Why were they torturing you? And how did you survive THAT??"

Josh's brain felt like it was going to explode: he couldn't believe that he had actually *watched* Rabboni die.

Rabboni looked around and spotted a marble seat in the garden. He then motioned for Josh to sit down beside him. Together they sat and talked until late. When Josh's eyelids were getting really heavy, Rabboni announced that it was time to "call it a night", and led Josh back to the Villa's entrance.

Somehow, Josh found his way back to his room, and literally dropped on top of his bed covers. His heart was burning with excitement.

It was all too much; it seemed too good to be true… Not surprisingly, it took ages to fall asleep on this particular night.

CHAPTER 38: THE PRODIGAL SON

Ally was pretty pleased with Brendan's progress. In about a week, he had mastered the English alphabet and could now read actual words. Ally was so delighted with Brendan's development that she was tempted to also teach him a bit of Italian. She had studied Italian at School, and felt confident Brendan could pick it up, but at the same time, Ally began to wonder what benefit Italian would be to him here...

In the late part of the morning, after chores were completed, the two of them would start their official lessons. Brendan enjoyed his private tuition immensely, and seemed to absorb new words like a "sponge". Sometimes, though, when Ally asked him to revise an "old" lesson, he would demonstrate his annoyance by defiantly folding up his arms and refusing to utter a single word. Mostly, though, Brendan was a willing and eager pupil, much to his Teacher's surprise.

Each lesson, though, began in the same way: "When's Josh coming back?" Brendan would ask in all seriousness, hoping that the answer today would be different.

"Soon, I hope," Ally routinely responded.

"C'mon, what does this say?" Ally began, writing the word *fish* on the dirt patch.

In actual fact, Ally shared Brendan's curiosity (and concern) about their brother's fate. It had been *ages* since Josh had left the Village in search of Rabboni, and there had been no sign of him since.

Imma, did not seem to be overly concerned by the boys' prolonged absence – but then again, Imma didn't have much time to worry about such things. Even with Ally's help, Imma worked from morning until night grinding grain, milking animals, baking bread, making cheese… and then there was the cleaning.

Ally's thoughts inevitably drifted to Aaron, as they tended to do each day. Soon after their private conversation, Aaron had been sent to a distant city on "business". Ally thought that the timing was a little *sus*…however, regional trade did appear to be an important part of the family's income.

It turned out that Aaron was invaluable to his Dad. Apparently, Aaron could speak multiple languages, making him the ideal candidate to deal with people of different nationalities. Aaron was also good at maths; at any time, he could work out the market value of fish and the distribution of income "shares". Not a simple task.

Ally couldn't stop thinking about him. The way Aaron looked at her, his tanned, muscular body… she even loved the way he smelled.

It's crazy, she mused, shuddering a little.

Suddenly, Ally was grabbed from behind in a bear hug.

"Hey Ally. We're BACK!"

Startled, Ally turned around to see Josh, grinning broadly.

"Josh! My God. Where have you been? I've been so worried," she admonished him while returning the hug. (Ally had never embraced Josh before, but today, she did it without even thinking about it.)

"I know. It's been a while… But it was worth it. Listen, Ally… I found Rabboni. That's not his real name, by the way… but he told me SO many things. Ally, I know how to get us back home!" Josh declared.

Hearing the excitement, Brendan raced out of the house and ran head-first into Josh's legs – he almost knocked him over with his enthusiasm.

"Hey, Brendan! It's good to see you, too, bro. Mate, have you grown?" Josh joked around with his little brother, ruffling his longish hair, while trying to stay upright in all the commotion.

"Where have you been Josh?" Brendan asked crossly. He stopped jumping for the briefest of moments in order to hear Josh's answer, but then changed his mind. "I waited and waited and you never came. I missed you. Now I have my whole family back!" Brendan happily announced, dancing a little jig before them.

Ally thought about how quickly Brendan had assimilated into Village life, effectively finding suitable "substitutes" for his real Mum and Dad within a relatively short space of time.

"Don't you want to see ALL your family again, Brendan?" Josh asked his brother in a serious tone.

Ally thought this was a dangerous question to pose to a little kid, especially if Josh couldn't deliver... Brendan thought for a moment, and then confided:

"I don't want to go back to our old house. There was too much fighting there. I thought we packed up and left our old country...to come to a new place and have a new life...where we love each other!" Brendan looked at his siblings, a little sheepishly.

Josh's eyes met Ally's. They had no idea that Brendan felt this way about their former life. It was true that the children had certainly entered a new country and found a new life within it; a land surprisingly filled with loving-kindness…

After Josh had cleaned himself up, he tried to speak to Ally privately. Sensing his need to talk, Ally left what she was doing and followed Josh into the garden. When they got to a shady spot, Josh turned to her and asked:

"Are you ready to go home, Ally?"

Ally looked at her brother, and hesitated before asking:

"Is that even possible, Josh?"

"Yes, it is." His whole face radiated with joy.

CHAPTER 39: WHATSHISNAME

"Ally, when I found him, it was incredible." Josh began. "Actually, HE found me, but the point is we talked for ages. He knew everything about me… He knew everything I ever did, from when I was a kid; about Mum and Dad, Melbourne… everything! Ally, he knows about ALL of us - inside and out!"

"I gather you're talking about Rabboni?" Ally asked him diffidently.

"Yes, but that's not his real name. Ally, wait for it…remember, back in Melbourne, in the church that day, when we all concentrated hard to find God? Well, God answered us… that day actually. Ally, he sent us his SON … Rabboni is God's son!"

Ally examined her brother closely, to see if he was kidding around. He looked completely serious.

"Ally, God's son became flesh and blood, and moved into THIS neighbourhood. Sometimes I can't believe it myself…but it's true, from start to finish. Ally, we saw him with our own eyes… And it turns out that God's son is just like his

Father…generous inside and out!" Josh said with deep conviction.

"What are you talking about?" Ally was completely lost.

"Ally, He gave up his life for us. I saw it happen. I was there."

Ally was aware of the sudden change in Josh's face, as he recounted a distressing event.

"I don't get it. Are you saying that Rabboni (or whoever he is) died?" she asked her brother gently.

"Well, yes and no. It's true that he died… I stood around with other people, and watched him die. But then God raised him back to life, and that's when he found me and we talked." Josh's animated expression returned.

"So, you're saying that Rabboni first died… or suicided, or whatever…then came alive again? Josh, that doesn't really make any sense. And even if I did believe what you're telling me, I don't see what it has to do with us."

"Ally, he died because he wanted US to have a real life, a better life, both now and in the future… He really loves us Ally."

"Josh, I know that things were a bit crap at home, but life was not *that* bad…" Ally responded flippantly.

Josh stopped abruptly and just stared at her. He was puzzled. Had Ally really forgotten about the way things were?

"Are you kidding me? Ally, how could you just wipe it from your memory? Back home, no-one talked, as much as yelled at each other. We were more like strangers, than a family… We just shared the same house."

Actually, there were lots of things Josh could've reminded Ally of, to prove his point, but something prevented him from continuing. (He couldn't bring himself to inflict further pain on her.)

In the seconds that followed, Ally became grim-faced as the dark memories gradually came flooding back to her.

"Brendan, where are you?" she called out with urgency.

"Here I am!" Brendan came racing out of nowhere, completely out of breath (like usual).

"Do you want me to do some more 'words'?" he asked excitedly.

Brendan was keen to demonstrate his new skills in front of his big brother.

"No, we're not doing words right now. We've got to do something else. Something important."

Looking at Josh, before taking a deep breath, Ally announced decisively:

"We're going home."

"But I don't want to go. I want to stay here!" Brendan became agitated. "PLEASE can we stay?" He implored them, his upper lip trembling slightly, as the tears began to cloud his worried eyes.

Ally bent down to cradle Brendan's head in her hands: "Brendan, I promise you, things will be different. *I* am going to be different. This time… I'm going to love you," Ally said momentously as tears streamed down her cheeks.

Josh then put his arms around both Ally and Brendan and held them close.

When they had composed themselves, the children went to find Imma and Jacob. They wanted to say "good-bye" properly and to express their immense gratitude for everything…

The family had given the children more than a place to stay. They had given them love. (Remarkably, the children didn't need to perform, or reach a certain standard to receive that love. It was there for the taking.)

One by one, the children conveyed their heartfelt thanks for the kindness that had been bestowed to them. When it was her turn to say goodbye, Ally embraced Imma and held on for a long time. She hoped that Imma understood that *this* was forever; she also wanted Imma to convey to Aaron *how much* Ally had cared for him.

Imma kissed all the children and they cried openly. Jacob cried too. For Imma and Jacob, the children were no longer strangers or foreigners, but proper members of their household - just as if they had been adopted.

When the final good-byes had been made, the children wandered off to a quiet spot, waiting for Josh to reveal what he knew.

"He said, 'You can ask for anything, using my name, and I will do it, for this will bring praise to the Father because of what I, the Son, will do for you.'" Josh declared unequivocally.

"OK...So, what's his name, then?" asked Ally, with great curiosity.

CHAPTER 40: NIGHT AT THE MUSEUM

"Jesus Christ! This is the perfect dress for you, Ally. We WON'T find another dress that hides your problem areas…" her mother snarled, careful not to be overheard by the pretty, young shop assistant.

Cassie was clearly annoyed with her stepdaughter for not agreeing with *her* choice of an evening dress. The dance was right around the corner, and Ally was being obstinate (and stupid) in Cassie's opinion. Cassie had sacrificed the best part of her weekend to help Ally find the right outfit, and instead of Ally being appreciative (of both her styling advice and the time she had invested) she was being *so* difficult.

"Mum, the dress is ok, but it's a bit too…. revealing for me," Ally responded shyly, hoping that her Stepmother could understand that the dress' low neckline made her feel really uncomfortable.

Cassie, however, had a yoga class in half an hour. She had to wrap this shopping trip up NOW. This was *no* time for false modesty, in Cassie's opinion.

"Rubbish. Your chest is your best feature. You need to accentuate what little you have, sweetie," she purred menacingly, stealing a final look at the fashion couture, to see what she might like for herself, as she began waving her MasterCard before the bemused shop assistant.

"Ok, Mum…. if you think it's the best one, we'll go with it," Ally finally consented, secretly hoping that she might *begin* to like the dress (once she walked around in it, within the privacy of her bedroom).

The children had been back for a few weeks now, and apart from a casual remark about their tanned complexions, their parents had not even realised they had been missing. At first, Josh and Ally had worried about how they were going to explain their absence to everyone, but they needn't have worried at all; the children had simply re-entered normal life, without missing a single second.

It appeared that instead of having *lost* time, the children had *gained* time… It was totally weird, according to Josh. He started to imagine that maybe the world and everything in it was not bound by limitations of time and space.

Ally did not have the time to think about such things. She had not being "asked" to the dance since they had returned home, and it was ALL that people were talking about. Finally, one of her friends had agreed to "share" her boyfriend. This arrangement suited Ally perfectly, especially when she learnt that Jack might be escorting at least three girls to the dance… (Ally wouldn't be the only one without her own partner.)

Her Stepmother, on the other hand, had been hugely disappointed that Ally had not been able to commandeer her own date, but mercifully, had left that subject unexplored, for now. Cassie seemed to be transfixed on the question of "evening wear".

The School had hired an events room at the Melbourne Museum for the annual dance, and everyone was eagerly looking forward to it…

When the day finally arrived, Ally was more than a little excited. Her Dad dropped her off at Bella's house, as Bella's Mum and older sisters would be doing the girls' hair and makeup.

"WOW, you look AWESOME!" Bella screamed when she opened her front door.

"Same!" Ally laughed, as Bella twirled around to show off her dress' pearl-beaded back seam.

Maddie arrived shortly after, and the house was soon replete with giggling and excitement.

"I've never seen so many beautiful women in one place," Bella's Dad declared, beaming with pride.

"Yes, you have. The girls are often over here," Bella's Mum corrected him good-naturedly.

But she knew what he meant. *The girls looked so amazingly grown-up.*

Each young woman was fussed over by the various members of Bella's household, and the "final touches" were then added by Bella's Mum.

When Jack finally arrived, he looked a little overwhelmed to be surrounded by so many *hot-looking chicks*.

"I've got my own harem!" Jack joked nervously, looking across at Bella's Dad.

"Hey, the others are only 'on loan', just this once," retorted Bella, pinching his middle affectionately.

When everyone had finished taking photos, Bella's Dad drove the group to the Dance and even parked the car, in order to escort the girls out properly, pretending to be a professional chauffeur.   He made everyone laugh, including Jack.

The Museum's entrance had been lined with plush red carpet, making the revellers feel like real celebrities. Jack double-backed on the carpet runner, insisting on walking each of his "dates" along the elegant red strip. The girls looked at one another and roared with laughter.

When they were all finally inside, they observed a huge foyer with polished concrete floors and glass cabinets containing interesting objects. Apparently, there was a special exhibition in progress which celebrated the identity, history and culture of the Jewish people.

As Ally's friends made their way through the crowd, they were greeted by other kids from School. *Everyone* was there. They each accepted a "mocktail" offered to them by a white-gloved waiter, and then just stood around, taking in the scene.

A short introduction was then made by the Museum staff, welcoming the teenagers to what promised to be an amazing night. The Curator encouraged the teens to examine the historic and contemporary artwork and objects "on loan, all the way from Jerusalem."

As Ally cast her eye around the exhibition, her heart skipped a beat. She actually recognised the pottery, the lamps, the jar rims with egg-and-dart decoration, the scale-weights... Ally automatically started to think about the "proper" way to wash these cups and copper bowls as Imma had taught her, and other bits of "melachot" (work).

Ally stepped closer to the objects and began to read the central billboard which contained the "introduction" to the Exhibition: *As the Jewish race sought to live a life of spiritual purity by strictly following the Jewish law or Torah, there were few pieces of art created. Their law strictly forbade them from making an idol in any form at all, whether man or woman, animal or bird, reptile or fish or constellations in the sky, as these would compete with their worship of their (one) true God. Consequently, the historic decorative items that have survived today are exceptionally rare.*

"Ally, you have GOT to look at this!"

Maddie grabbed Ally forcibly by the hand and frog-marched her over to an area which was getting a lot of foot traffic. Ally pushed her way through the crowd, and there it was....

The accompanying card read:

Origin: Discovered in a rubble collapse of an early Roman period dwelling, circa 1st century.

Image: Portrait of a Young Jewish girl with her hair in a bun.

Title: Beloved

Point of Interest: Note the pendant worn by the young woman which strangely depicts the Country of Australia surrounded by the Indian and Pacific Oceans? The image of Australia would normally date the picture to post 1770 (when Australia was claimed by Great Britain.) However, using scientific radiocarbon dating plus evidence of the ochre crayons used to make the artwork, archaeologists have authenticated the item as belonging to the first century.

The picture was of Ally.

CHAPTER 41: PAW (PARENTS ARE WATCHING)

Ally didn't remember much after that. Somehow, Ally had fended off the inevitable questions and the raised eyebrows from many curious onlookers. The resemblance was uncanny… but how could Ally possibly explain to anyone what *she* was doing in that picture? She could barely understand it herself.

One thing she was certain of, however, was that she had been loved. The thought of Aaron made her heart soar.

The next day was Sunday. Ordinarily, Ally would have slept in, but when she woke, she could not stop thinking about what had happened last night. Ally decided she might as well get up and start breakfast. As she began preparing the pancake mixture, Josh appeared in his PJs.

"Hey, how was the dance?" he asked enthusiastically, as he searched for the frying pan.

"Really good. What topping should we have?" Ally was trying to act cool, in spite of the events of the last twenty-four hours.

"MMMmmmm…how about red grapes sweetened with honey? And some cinnamon of course." Josh began salivating.

"Sounds good. Anyway, you'll NEVER guess what I saw," Ally began teasing him.

"I'll tell you what I can see." Cassie suddenly walked in with an unmistakeable frown on her face - she was clearly not impressed with the current state of her Ceasarstone benchtop.

"I can see a huge mess! That's all I can see… This kitchen better be left the way you found it Ally," she threatened, shuffling past them in her slippers as she prepared to make herself some strong coffee.

"Of course, Mum. By the way, how many pancakes do you want?" Josh asked, winking at Ally.

Cassie hesitated: "One will do me…thanks," she muttered, in an altogether gentler tone.

Once the coffee machine was doing its "thing," Cassie turned around to study the children. She couldn't work it out, but Josh appeared to be different… more confident somehow. Well, he was (after all) her natural offspring, she concluded haughtily.

"So how was last night?" Cassie glanced at her stepdaughter, yawning as she waited for a response. "What did you SEE?"

"It was pretty awesome actually. The dance was held in the Museum (as you know) so there was lots of artwork and interesting stuff everywhere," Ally answered truthfully.

"And…what was Bella wearing? Did you get to dance with anyone?" Cassie probed.

"Bella looked amazing. I'll show you some photos later…We all kind of danced together, so it was pretty cool, you know…" Ally hoped her Step-Mum would be satisfied with this response.

"What's for breakfast?" Brendan suddenly appeared, carrying his new Tram toy with him.

"Pancakes. You want some?" Ally asked him playfully.

"YES, PLEASE!" Brendan shrieked excitedly.

"INSIDE VOICE, please!" Cassie chastised.

"Can you make them like Imma used to?" Brendan asked his sister.

Josh and Ally both looked in the direction of their mother, to see whether she had heard…

"Who's Imma?" their Father asked as he sauntered in, making a beeline for the freshly brewed coffee.

"What are you talking about?" Cassie asked her husband, as she offered him a mug.

"Someone said something about 'Imma', but then again, my brain hasn't had its official kick-start yet."

Brett gulped down the caffeine; his attempt at humour falling a little flat.

Josh looked at his father, and suddenly realised how sad and lonely he looked. His father actually reminded him of Jonathon.

"Dad, would you like me and Brendan to help you with the garden today?"

Brett looked at Josh in surprise, and muttered something about the garden desperately needing some attention.

"Ok, then… after breakfast, we'll all get cracking," Josh announced.

"What's gotten into you kids? You're all acting very strangely," declared Cassie, while she stole a look at her husband, and met a similar look of disbelief.

"We're not strange, Mummy. We're a FAM-ILY. Families help each other," Brendan explained, looking earnestly at his Mum.

"Well… out of the mouth of babes!" Cassie exclaimed, clearly impressed by the wisdom of her youngest child.

When the boys had finally finished devouring their golden pancakes and licking the final bit of honey off their lips, they changed into some casual shorts, and went outside to find their Dad.

It was a perfectly-crisp morning. Standing in the overgrown garden, still covered with morning dew (and the promise of a beautiful day ahead), Josh couldn't help looking up and marvelling:

"God, your greatness is seen in all the world! When I look at the sky which you have made, at the moon and the stars, which you set in their places - what are human beings that you think of them; and even kids, that you care for them?"

But Josh knew that God did care for him and for his family. From the very beginning of time itself, HE was there. Josh was confident that God would *always* be there for them.

As long as he lived, Josh would never forget what he had seen with his own eyes… One day, he would even tell his children and grandchildren about the day he had stood in the presence of the living God.

244

THE END

www.ingramcontent.com/pod-product-compliance
Lightning Source LLC
Chambersburg PA
CBHW070442120726
47910CB00003B/893